U0006762

喚醒你的英文語感！

Get a Feel for English !

喚醒你的英文語感！

Get a Feel for English !

EMI in Online Classrooms

雙語課室
英文句典

作者 ◎ 薛詠文　　　推薦 ◎ 國立陽明交通大學
　　　　　　　　　　　　　英語教學研究所暨語言教學與研究中心
　　　　　　　　　　　　　孫于智 教授兼所長

課堂必學語句　教學互動溝通　作業評量指導　線上課程應用

I'm sharing the syllabus. Do you all see it on the screen now?
You'll find readings related to the lectures on the class website.
I've established a LINE group for this course, so please scan this QR code to enter.

貝塔語言出版
Beta Multimedia Publishing

H·EDU
高等教育

　　因應政府頒訂「2030 雙語國家政策」,「英語授課」一詞近年來成為教育界各階層(從國小到研究所)最受關注的議題之一。而對國內多數教師而言,以英語作為課堂的主要溝通語言確實是一大挑戰。本書的推出,無疑是教師們可「現學現用」的利器,透過研讀、不斷練習及活用本書完整的架構與精選例句,教師們必定能一步步將原本不甚熟稔的課室英語,逐漸轉化成自然而然脫口而出的教學用語。

　　本書主要分為六大單元,完整涵蓋課程簡介、講課、評量、師生互動、學生間的交流等。最令人驚豔的是第一單元的「線上課室基本用語」,其內容針對疫情時代下的線上教學需求,支援教師們莫大幫助。本書特色包含列舉核心單字的中文解釋與詞性註記,「Useful Tips」專欄則收錄了教師在講授該單元項目時的溫馨提醒。這些溫馨提醒皆為作者累積多年教學經驗的心得菁華,不僅可提供教師授課的參考,對學生的學習亦頗有助益。

　　《雙語課室英文句典》是一本英語授課的寶典工具書。不僅適合在職及預備從事英語授課的各級學校、各類領域之教師應用;單字註記內容也讓本書成為學生修習英語課程的先備教材,是英語課程教科書籍的最佳選擇。藉由教師引導學生熟悉英語授課所必須經歷的各項聽講和課堂活動,讓學生預習相關英語表達、詞彙的使用,對於之後適應英語課堂可收顯著之成效。

本書作者薛詠文是一位資深講師，專長爲英語授課、雙語教學及知識與內容整合學習 (Content and Language Integrated Learning, CLIL)。薛老師屢屢受邀於國內各大學、專科以下學校進行學術和教學講座，其擁有美國 Fairleigh Dickinson University 資訊工程碩士學位，基於對英語教學的熱愛，目前就讀於國立陽明交通大學英語教學所，在校成績表現優異，是書卷獎得主。近年並受邀於陽明交通大學外語進修班開設課程，其教學功力和熱忱廣受學生們愛戴與肯定。本書乃集結薛老師多年的教學經驗及紮實的學術涵養，精心彙整精簡、易上手的英語授課好學好用短句，相信必能嘉惠眾多投入 2030 雙語國家願景的所有師生。

國立陽明交通大學
英語教學研究所暨語言教學與研究中心
教授兼所長

近幾年來，不論是各級學校教師亦或家長，在聽到「政府推動雙語教育」或「力促台灣打造雙語環境」等議題時，所持的態度有兩極化的呈現。

有抱持正面態度樂觀其成的一派，認為台灣在科技、經濟與文化層面上早已與國際接軌並環環相扣，推動國際語言——英語——的學習與精進本是理所應當之事。相反地，也有人偏悲觀地認為如此的政策無疑是 "mission impossible"（不可能的任務）且實施上困難重重，教師本身「以英語授課」之能力尚未培養成氣候之際就要進行教學，恐造成學子觀念混淆避坑落井，英文本身沒學好不說，恐怕連學科知識都被犧牲了。

雙方的論點聽來皆頗有道理，不知讀者各位的想法為何？

筆者認為，的確萬事起頭難，但是自政府發佈「推行雙語教育」、「打造英語環境」的那一刻起，此事便已非教師或學生喜不喜歡或想不想做的問題了，師生所需的其實就是一股「共同精進」、「非做不可」的魄力，讓不可能變為可能。

當然，要配合達成「2030 雙語國家政策」的艱鉅目標也不是光靠信心喊話就可實現的。身在教育前線的教師們必須付諸具體行動，一步一腳印地積累自身實力，除了本身所教授的專業領域知識之外，若能再搭配上紮實的英語授課能力，真可謂如虎添翼，不僅嘉惠學子，更著實增添了教師自身與時俱進的價值。

再者，雙語目標的實踐也並非僅由教師唱獨角戲即可，不光是教師的責任，從某種程度來看，其實學生才是重要的 "stakeholders"（利益相關者）呢！新時代的學生應調整學習心境與態度，從傳統「等教師餵知識」的被動心態，提升到「培養主動求知的精神」才有能力在競爭激烈的二十一世紀斬獲成功。

目前在台灣實行的雙語教育可分兩大主軸，分別為國／高中較適用的 CLIL（Content and Language Integrated Learning 學科語言整合學習），以及大專院校的 EMI（English as a Medium of Instruction 全英授課），但不論是以哪種方式進行雙語教學，各級教師皆需要運用到大量的課室英語 (Classroom English) 以維持和學生的雙向溝通。有鑑於此，既然師生都需要為今後雙語教育環境做準備，本書的編輯初衷與應用便可在此刻發揮強大的功效。為了協助教師與學生在英語授課的道路上更順利地進入狀況，本書以雙語課室內的各式情境作分類，不僅列出了教師們可立即派上用場的核心語句，也囊括了學生互動與提問等情境對白。

另外值得一提的是，因應「遠距學習已成為後疫情新常態」的趨勢，本書更著重於處理線上課程所需的實用短語，從技術問題疑難排解到雲端授課等主題皆完整收錄。為避免過於冗長或須經背頌而致口語表達上顯得生硬呆板，所有語句的挑選與設計皆以精簡、活用為主，讓教師與學生們可在短期內精進熟練且多加練習揣摩後自然地朗朗上口。

更重要的是，現今已有不少雙語種子教師被學校要求須通過標準化英檢認證（TOEFL / IELTS 等）以證明具備 B2[註] 或以上的英語能力。（或是學生至少須具備 A1[註] 以上的英語能力等。）而這些英檢考試不免會包括口說與寫作的評測，著眼於此現狀，本書更特別規劃了 "BONUS" 單元，以「討論線上課程利弊」為主軸，歸納出口語討論與意見書寫的範例。

　　本書面面俱到，網羅實務上雙語課室的真實情境，側重後疫情新常態的遠距學習，編寫出實用率最高的英文教‧學雙向語句，並隨相應內容適時提供淬鍊於筆者親身經驗的教學指引，期望能協助師生雙方在雙語課室有更加順暢的體驗並收事半功倍之效。

薛詠文

註：B2 等級是依據語言能力評量標準 CEFR（Common European Framework of Reference for Languages 歐洲語言共同參考架構）。各類英檢成績參考對應表見 P.173。

本書附有 MP3 音檔和六大學科領域必備字彙補充帖，請刮開書內刮刮卡，上網啓用序號後即可下載聆聽使用。
網址：https://bit.ly/3d3P7te
或掃描 QR code

貝塔會員網

CONTENTS

Unit III Lectures 講課

Phrases for Online Classes

線上課室基本用語

☐ Good morning, everyone.
大家早安。

☐ Good afternoon, students.
同學們午安。

☐ Hello, everybody.
大家好。

☐ **Welcome**[1], everyone.
歡迎大家。

☐ How's everything?
一切都好嗎？

☐ How's everyone feeling today?
大家今天好嗎？

VOCABULARY

① welcome (*v.*) 歡迎

☐ How's everybody doing this morning?

大家今天早上都還好嗎？

☐ I hope you're all feeling well.

希望每個人都精神滿滿。

☐ I'd like to welcome you to this **online**[2] **course**[3].

歡迎各位參與此線上課程。

☐ I'm very **pleased**[4] to see you all online.

非常高興和你們在線上見面。

Useful Tips

首次在線上見面，教師免不了要先與學生們打個招呼。招呼用語並不會因為是實體課程或線上課程有太大差異，重點在於，若是線上課程，有可能尚未透過螢幕看到所有同學的影像，不比在實體班面對面地互動，在招呼的語氣上就得更加熱忱一些，以便藉由聲音讓同學感受得到。

VOCABULARY

② online (*adj.*) 線上的 (*adv.*) 在線上
③ course (*n.*) 課程
④ pleased (*adj.*) 開心的

檢查連線
Checking Connections

☐ Hey, Jessica. Can you hear me?

嗨，潔西卡。聽得到嗎？

☐ Can everybody hear me **clearly**[1]?

每個人都聽得清楚嗎？

☐ I think I've got a bad **connection**[2].

我的連線不太穩定。

☐ Let me **log out**[3] and try to **reconnect**[4].

我先登出再連一次看看。

☐ Yes, we can hear you **perfectly**[5].

可以，我們都聽得很清楚。

VOCABULARY

① clearly (*adv.*) 清楚地
② connection (*n.*) 連線；聯繫
③ log out 登出
④ reconnect (*v.*) 重新連線
⑤ perfectly (*adv.*) 完美地；圓滿地

▶ TRACK **02**

☐ All of you, please keep your mics on **mute**[6].

請大家將麥克風調靜音。

☐ Is the connection better now?

現在連線有較穩定了嗎？

☐ We've lost Jessica. **Hold on**[7] a second.

潔西卡斷線了。請等一下。

☐ John, you're **breaking up**[8].

約翰，你聽起來斷斷續續的耶。

☐ How about now? Is that clear?

現在呢？清楚點了嗎？

Useful Tips

線上連線不穩可能造成學生無法登入或聲音斷續等狀況，常見的描述除了 "I can't hear you." 之外，還可說 "We've lost [someone]."，其中動詞 lose 在此不要翻成「遺失」喔，其實就是「聽不見某人」(fail to hear someone) 之意。另，若聲音斷斷續續，可說 "You're breaking up."，其中片語 "break up" 在此是指「聲音聽不清楚」。

VOCABULARY

⑥ mute (*adj.*) 無聲的
⑦ hold on 等一下
⑧ break up 破碎；散開

☐ I can't hear you.

聽不到聲音。

☐ Please check if your mic is **plugged in**[1].

請檢查你的麥克風是否有插好。

☐ I hear a lot of **static**[2].

我一直聽到雜訊。

☐ I'm having a sound **issue**[3]. Hold on a second.

我這邊聲音有些問題。請稍等。

☐ Jack, could you please **speak up**[4] a bit?

傑克，你可以講大聲點嗎？

☐ Your voice is a bit **loud**[5]. Can you **turn down**[6] your mic a bit?

你的聲音有點大。你可以把麥克風轉小聲點嗎？

VOCABULARY

① plug in 插入（插座）
② static (*n.*) 靜電；雜音
③ issue (*n.*) 問題
④ speak up 大聲點說
⑤ loud (*adj.*) 大聲的
⑥ turn down 關小聲

TRACK **03**

☐ Sorry, what was that? Could you say that again?

不好意思，你剛說什麼？可以再說一次嗎？

☐ Jack, could you **repeat**[7] what you just said?

傑克，你剛說什麼可以再講一次嗎？

☐ Linda, please have your mic **turned on**[8].

琳達，請將麥克風打開。

☐ How's my **voice**[9]? Any better?

現在聲音如何？好點了嗎？

Useful Tips

若因音源不佳，有需要請講者再重複所說的話，可說 "Could you say that again?" 或 "Do you mind saying it again?" 或 "Could you repeat that?"，但沒必要說 "Can you repeat it again?" 喔！因為 repeat 本身就是「重複」之意，不必再使用 again 一字強調。

○**VOCABULARY**

⑦ repeat (*v.*) 重複
⑧ turn on 開啟
⑨ voice (*n.*) 聲音 (*v.*)（用言語）表達

☐ Now I can see you guys. I just had to change a few **settings**[1].

現在我可以看到各位了。我稍微調了一些設定就 OK 了。

☐ Is Daniel here? Oh, no. We lost Daniel.

丹尼爾在嗎？不會吧，丹尼爾離線了。

☐ It seems like Jessica is **cutting out**[2].

看來潔西卡是斷線了。

☐ John, are you still with us? I can't see you.

約翰，你還在線上嗎？我沒看到你耶。

☐ All right. We've got everyone here already. Let's start the lesson.

好的，全部的人都在線上了。我們就開始上課吧。

☐ I'm **sharing**[3] the **syllabus**[4]. Do you all see it on the **screen**[5] now?

我將課程表分享出來，大家都有在螢幕上看到嗎？

○ **VOCABULARY**

① setting (*n.*) 設定
② cut out 停止；斷線
③ share (*v.*) 分享
④ syllabus (*n.*) 課程大綱
⑤ screen (*n.*) 螢幕

◯ TRACK **04**

☐ Michael, could you make your **slides**[6] bigger please?

麥可，可以請你把投影片放大一點嗎？

☐ Mary, you can change your **background**[7] if you'd like.

瑪麗，妳如果想更換背景也是可以。

☐ I'm sorry. My **webcam**[8] is not working.

不好意思，我的攝影鏡頭怪怪的。

☐ Joe, would you like to share your screen with us?

喬，你想分享你的螢幕嗎？

Useful Tips

實務上進行線上課程時，常聽同學說 "I can't open my webcam."，這樣的話便是直接用 "open"「開」一字直譯了「開鏡頭」，但 open 是指「開啟」，正確而言應使用片語 "turn on" 表「打開」、「啟用」之意；要請同學將鏡頭打開則可說 "Please have your webcam turned on."。

VOCABULARY

⑥ slide (*n.*) 投影片
⑦ background (*n.*) 背景
⑧ webcam (*n.*) 網路攝影機

☐ Okay, I'm going to send you the **invite**[1] again.
好的,我會把邀請連結再寄一次給你。

☐ Please key in the access code: XUI-TGS.
請輸入代碼:XUI-TGS。

☐ You should **download**[2] the most recent **version**[3] of the **application**[4].
你要下載最新版的應用軟體。

☐ You should try to **adjust**[5] your **output**[6] settings first.
你應先試著調整輸出的設定。

☐ Oops, my bad. I was on mute. Let me just start over.
噢,不好意思。我剛關靜音了。我再重講一次。

☐ Betty, do you see the **icon**[7] at top of the screen? **Click**[8] on it to share your screen.
貝蒂,妳有看到螢幕上方的圖示嗎?點一下就可以分享螢幕了。

☐ If you have any questions, please click on the "Raise Hand" icon.
如果有任何問題,請點「舉手」按鍵。

VOCABULARY

① invite (*n.*) 邀請函 (*v.*) 邀請
② download (*v.*) 下載
③ version (*n.*) 版本
④ application (*n.*) 應用程式;申請(書)
⑤ adjust (*v.*) 調整
⑥ output (*n.*) 輸出
⑦ icon (*n.*)〔電腦〕圖示
⑧ click (*v.*) 點擊

☐ For some reason, my "Share Screen" icon is gone.

不知為何，我的「分享螢幕」按鈕不見了。

☐ Let me leave the meeting room for now and I'll **sign** back **in**[9] soon.

我現在先離開會議室一下，等等很快就會再登入。

☐ Linda, please check if you have **received**[10] an email invitation for our Zoom meeting.

琳達，請查看一下妳是否有收到 Zoom 會議的邀請函郵件。

Useful Tips

在協助上線學生排解軟硬體困難時，最重要的是要使用明確的語言。比方說，要請學生查看是否有看到某個按紐，避免模糊地說 "Do you see an icon there?"「你有沒看到一個按鍵？」，而應明確地說："Do you see a blue icon in the upper right corner?"「你在右上角有沒有看到一個藍色的按鍵？」，如此便可讓學生更有效率地操作。

VOCABULARY

⑨ sign in 登入
⑩ receive (v.) 收到；接收

☐ This 10-session course will be **conducted**[1] online using TeamX.

此十堂課程將會利用 TeamX 軟體在線上進行。

☐ I'll send you an invite via email, so please check your inbox to get the **link**[2] before class.

我會將邀請連結用電郵寄給大家,請在上課前檢視信箱以獲取連結。

☐ I **suggest**[3] that you join the class from a quiet location.

我建議你們找個安靜的地方來上課。

☐ I'm now sharing a slide on the screen. Click on the "Raise Hand" icon if you have a problem seeing it.

我已將投影片分享在螢幕上。看不到的人請點一下「舉手」圖示。

☐ If you have any questions or **comments**[4], feel free to **unmute**[5] your mic and **interrupt**[6] me.

如果有任何問題或意見,隨時歡迎開麥克風提出。

☐ Please feel free to leave your questions or comments in the "Message" box on the right side of the screen, and I'll try to **address**[7] them **immediately**[8].

如果有問題或意見要提出,可在螢幕右方的「訊息欄」內打下訊息,我會馬上回覆。

VOCABULARY

① conduct (*v.*) 處理;進行
② link (*n.*) 連結
③ suggest (*v.*) 建議
④ comment (*n.*) 評論;意見

⑤ unmute (*v.*) 重開聲音
⑥ interrupt (*v.*) 打斷
⑦ address (*v.*) 應付;處理
⑧ immediately (*adv.*) 立即;馬上

☐ If you're getting a black screen, that means you may have used the wrong login **credentials**[9].

你的螢幕如果全黑，那代表你登入資訊錯誤。

☐ Please **ensure**[10] the username and password you are entering are **correct**[11].

請確認你登入的帳號、密碼都正確。

☐ Jessie, what **error**[12] **message**[13] are you getting? Please read it to me.

潔希，妳看到什麼錯誤訊息？請唸給我聽。

☐ I'll **divide** you guys **into**[14] five groups for discussion activities.

我會將你們分為五組以進行討論活動。

Useful Tips

線上課程雖說也可透過電腦螢幕看到參與者影像，但事實上和實體課程的互動還是有差異的。因此，開始線上課程之前，教師應事先說明線上課程的互動方式。比方說，教師是希望同學麥克風關靜音以避免干擾？還是希望開著麥克風隨時準備回答問題？又比方說討論問題時，是個人回答？還是分組討論？這些細節的指引應在線上課程開始之前就讓同學瞭解。

VOCABULARY

⑨ credential (*n.*) 憑證
⑩ ensure (*v.*) 確認；確保
⑪ correct (*adj.*) 正確的

⑫ error (*n.*) 錯誤
⑬ message (*n.*) 訊息
⑭ divide into 分開；分成

☐ Welcome to the class. Let's work together to make this an enjoyable online learning experience for everyone.

歡迎來上課。讓我們一起讓這個線上學習課程變得愉快有趣。

☐ In the meantime, I'll mute all **participants**[1].

我現在會先將大家都關靜音。

☐ During the class, I'll be writing formulas on the whiteboard, so please follow along closely.

課程當中我會將數學公式都寫在白板上,請仔細地跟上。

☐ I'll allow some time for you to **reflect**[2] and ask questions.

我會留點時間讓大家反思和提問。

☐ Please have your webcams turned on so that we can interact as normally as possible.

請將你們的網路攝影機打開以便我們討論互動。

☐ The school has set up a shared **folder**[3] for us to use. Once you've finished your homework **assignments**[4], please **upload**[5] the **files**[6] there.

學校已設定了共享資料夾給同學使用。你們完成作業後,請將檔案上傳到那邊。

VOCABULARY

① participant (*n.*) 參與者
② reflect (*v.*) 反映;表達
③ folder (*n.*) 文件夾
④ assignment (*n.*) 指派任務;作業
⑤ upload (*v.*) 上傳
⑥ file (*n.*) 檔案

⊙ TRACK **07**

☐ Okay, now let's review lessons using Kahoot!, which is a game-based learning **platform**[7].

好的,現在我們透過遊戲學習平台 Kahoot! 來複習一下學過的課程。

☐ We're going to use Padlet for our online sessions. So, first I'm going to show you how it works, okay?

我們的線上課程會使用 Padlet。首先,我來示範給你們看要如何操作。

☐ The first step is to create a **virtual**[8] "Wall," which is an **interactive**[9] space where you can **post**[10] **texts**[11], **images**[12], and even files.

第一步是要建立一個虛擬的「牆面」,然後你就可以貼文字、圖像甚至檔案到此互動空間上。

☐ What I want you to do now is discuss the questions I gave you with your partners and then post your ideas on Padlet.

現在我要請你們做的是,跟夥伴討論我剛講的問題,並將你們的意見寫到 Padlet 上。

Useful Tips

線上課程缺乏直接的人際互動。因此,線上課程教師的責任之一是要善用線上工具來與學生互動。比方說,透過 google doc 共編文件,或是利用 Pear Deck、Kahoot!、Quizizz、Padlet 等工具跟學生有些交流。

VOCABULARY

⑦ platform (*n.*) 平台
⑧ virtual (*adj.*) 虛擬的
⑨ interactive (*adj.*) 互動的
⑩ post (*v.*) 張貼
⑪ text (*n.*) 文字;本文
⑫ image (*n.*) 圖像

☐ Now, I'd like you to work in groups.

現在我想請大家分組討論。

☐ I'll **enable**[1] **breakout**[2] rooms for you. Jenny and Mark, you're in group A, so please click the first link. Linda and Tom, you're in group B, so click on the second link, please.

我幫大家設好分組討論室。珍妮和馬克,你們倆是 A 組,所以要點第一個連結。琳達和湯姆,你們是 B 組,請點第二個連結。

☐ You could also set up your own meeting rooms to talk with your classmates.

你們也可以開啟自己的會議室跟同學討論。

☐ This is a group activity. I'm going to give you ten minutes to **brainstorm**[3] ideas.

這是個分組活動。我會給你們十分鐘腦力激盪一下點子。

☐ After you've finished, please click on the **original**[4] link and rejoin the main classroom.

你們討論完之後,請點原本的連結,再加回到主教室。

☐ I suggest you choose a **group**[5] **leader**[6] first.

我建議你們先選個組長。

VOCABULARY

① enable (v.) 授與……能力
② breakout (adj.) 〔會議〕分組的
③ brainstorm (v.) 腦力激盪

④ original (adj.) 原始的;原本的
⑤ group (n.) 小組 (v.) 分組
⑥ leader (n.) 領導者

⊡ TRACK **08**

☐ The tasks I want you to work on are already posted on Padlet.

我要你們做的任務都已貼在 Padlet 平台上。

☐ All the discussion questions are **available**[7] on Google Drive, so please make sure you have **access**[8] to the link.

所有要討論的問題都在 Google 雲端硬碟上了，請確認你們可以存取此連結。

☐ All right, it seems like everyone is back. Could each group please share what they discussed?

好的，看來大家都已回到教室。每組可以跟我們分享一下討論結果嗎？

☐ Group one, please share with us what **solutions**[9] you've come up with to the first problem on the list.

第一組，請跟我們分享一下針對第一個問題你們討論出什麼解決方案。

Useful Tips

多數的線上會議工具都有「分組討論」的功能（有些工具可能要視會議召集人的權限而定），可善加利用。線上分組的人數通常以三到四位學生為最佳，以確保每人都有貢獻意見的機會。若非得有五人以上的小組討論，則討論時間就要拉長一些了。

○ VOCABULARY

⑦ available (*adj.*) 可取得的
⑧ access (*n.*) 存取權
⑨ solution (*n.*) 解決辦法

Notes

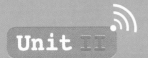

Unit II

Introductions

課程簡介

☐ Welcome to the class. Today we'll just go over some **general**[1] information together.

歡迎參加此課程。今天我們會一起討論課程資訊。

☐ This is a **required**[2] course for all students **majoring**[3] in business management.

這門課是所有商管學系同學的必修課。

☐ This is an **elective**[4] for anyone who needs to **improve**[5] their writing skills.

這是門選修課，想精進寫作技巧的同學都可加入。

☐ Let's go through some important **items**[6] listed in this syllabus, including the course schedule and homework assignments.

我們一起看一下課程表內的一些重要資訊，包括課程時間和指定作業等。

☐ The course is called Writing 11 and will mainly **focus on**[7] **academic**[8] writing.

這門課是「寫作 11」，主要會討論學術文章的撰寫。

☐ We'll meet once a week on Wednesday from 9 to 11. This course is **worth**[9] two **credits**[10].

我們一週上課一次，每週三的九點到十一點。這門課是兩學分的課程。

VOCABULARY

① general (*adj.*) 一般的
② required (*adj.*) 必要的；要求的
③ major (*v.*) 主修 (*n.*) 主修科目
④ elective (*n./adj.*) 選修課；選修的
⑤ improve (*v.*) 改善；增強
⑥ item (*n.*) 項目
⑦ focus on 聚焦於
⑧ academic (*adj.*) 學術的
⑨ worth (*adj.*) 有……價值的
⑩ credit (*n.*) 學分

TRACK **09**

☐ The **prerequisite**[11] for this course is English 21.

修這門課之前必須先修過 English 21。

☐ This is a class on machine learning. Specifically, we'll **explore**[12] some applications of artificial intelligence in the health care field.

這門課教的是機器學習。更精準地說,我們要探討人工智慧在健康管理產業的應用。

☐ This writing class is different from other creative writing classes because we will focus on creative nonfiction.

這門寫作課程與其他創意寫作課有所不同,因為我們會聚焦在寫真實的故事。

☐ We won't be covering data **analysis**[13] and **visualization**[14], so if that's what you're looking for, feel free to drop the class.

在這門課當中我們不會討論到資料分析和視覺化,所以假如不符合你的期待,可以退選。

Useful Tips

在介紹課程時,即使學生手邊有對應的 syllabus 大綱可參考,但這不意味著教師就用英文照著唸過去即可,而應根據要點使用順暢的「英文口語」自然地表達;建議使用「簡單易懂」的詞彙以便讓學生快速瞭解,避免一開始就使用高深單字或慣用語等混淆學生。

○ VOCABULARY

⑪ prerequisite (*n.*) 先決條件
⑫ explore (*v.*) 探索;研究
⑬ analysis (*n.*) 分析
⑭ visualization (*n.*) 視覺化

02

介紹課程目的
Introducing the Course Objectives

☐ All right, now we come to the important part. Let's talk about some of the **objectives**[1] of the course.

好的，現在我們要來討論重要的部分。讓我們談談此課程的一些目標。

☐ This writing course is not only about producing correct sentences, but also about writing **essays**[2] that **inspire**[3] people.

這門寫作課程不僅要教大家寫出正確的句子，更是要寫出可激勵人心的文章。

☐ We're going to cover a wide range of topics, from the history of **technology**[4] to some recent technological **developments**[5].

我們的課程將涵蓋廣泛的主題，從科技的歷史到現代科技發展。

☐ This semester, we're going to explore a few of the main approaches to machine learning **algorithms**[6].

在本學期，我們將探討機器學習演算法的原理。

☐ You'll have **acquired**[7] the ability to design a complete **website**[8] by the end of the class.

課程結束時，你們將具備設計完整網站的能力。

VOCABULARY

① objective (*n.*) 目的；目標
② essay (*n.*) 論述文
③ inspire (*v.*) 激勵；鼓舞
④ technology (*n.*) 科技
⑤ development (*n.*) 發展
⑥ algorithm (*n.*) 演算法
⑦ acquire (*v.*) 習得
⑧ website (*n.*) 網站

⊙ TRACK **10**

☐ After you enter the job market, you'll be able to **apply**[9] the **presentation**[10] skills taught in this class.

進入就業市場後，你們將能夠應用本課程中所教的演說技巧。

☐ After today's lesson, you will be able to write a persuasive four-paragraph opinion essay.

今天上完課後，你們將可寫出一篇具有說服力的四段式意見論述文。

☐ Our goal for this class is to teach you how to **develop**[11] an AI system.

此課程的目標是要教你們如何研發一套人工智慧系統。

☐ This is an **advanced**[12] biomedical engineering course.

這堂課是生物醫學工程的進階課程。

☐ Your grade will be determined by your presentation **performance**[13] and exam **scores**[14].

同學們的成績會根據簡報表現和考試成績來評定。

Useful Tips

在介紹課程目標時，建議可多利用 "After this class, you will be able to demonstrate ... [some goals]." 此句型。

VOCABULARY

⑨ apply (*v.*) 應用
⑩ presentation (*n.*) 簡報
⑪ develop (*v.*) 開發；發展

⑫ advanced (*adj.*) 進階的
⑬ performance (*n.*) 表現
⑭ score (*n.*) 分數

☐ Let's start today's lesson by talking about some of the papers that you'll have to read.

今天課程一開始，我們就先來講一下你們需要讀的文章。

☐ If you're interested in exploring more about the history of technology, this book is fairly **comprehensive**[1].

如果你對探討更多關於科技發展的歷史有興趣，本書內有詳盡的介紹。

☐ If you'd like to jump right into the section on future developments, please go directly to chapter 6.

如果你想直接看關於未來發展的部分，可直接跳到第六章。

☐ You may find it a bit **challenging**[2] to read this book in English, but I'll **provide**[3] a **vocabulary**[4] list and PowerPoint slides to help you.

同學可能會認為閱讀英文版課本有點困難，但我會提供詞彙表和投影片來協助你們。

☐ You'll also be required to read at least three **journal articles**[5] of your own choice.

同學們還需要閱讀至少三篇自選的期刊文章。

☐ I've also shared some other technology-related websites and **video**[6] links on our Google Classroom Classwork page.

我還在 Google Classroom Classwork 頁面上分享了一些與科技相關的網站和影片連結。

VOCABULARY

① comprehensive (*adj.*) 全面的
② challenging (*adj.*) 具挑戰性的
③ provide (*v.*) 提供
④ vocabulary (*n.*) 詞彙
⑤ journal article 期刊
⑥ video (*n.*) 影片

◉ TRACK **11**

☐ All **pre-recorded**[7] videos are available online. Let me post a link to them in the chat box.

所有預錄的影片都放在雲端上了。我將連結貼在聊天區。

☐ I've established a LINE group for this course, so please **scan**[8] this QR code to enter.

我為課程建了一個 LINE 群組，掃描這個 QR code 便可加入。

☐ I'll post ten **extra**[9] reading articles in our class page on Facebook. Please make sure you can access them.

我會在臉書上的班級社團上貼十篇額外的閱讀文章，請確認一下你們可存取資料。

☐ Additional audio files will be provided on our course website.

額外的音檔會放在我們的課程網站上。

Useful Tips

在資訊多元化的年代，可提供給學生的教材也不僅限於課本了，而是還可能包括影片、音檔、文章、網站資訊等，若能整合些後續讓同學實際操作的 hands-on 活動，效果將可加倍。比方說請同學看完影片後做一分鐘的口頭報告，或閱讀文章後填寫相關 worksheet 回答問題、寫出摘要……等都是能夠協助同學內化知識的活動。

VOCABULARY

⑦ pre-recorded (*adj.*) 事先錄好的
⑧ scan (*v.*) 掃描
⑨ extra (*adj.*) 額外的

☐ The **textbook**[1] we'll use throughout the semester is *Writing Trainer*, **authored**[2] by Dr. Rachel Lee.

在此學期我們會使用的教科書是《寫作培訓師》，其作者為李瑞秋博士。

☐ This book is written by Dr. Cole Jones, a leading **expert**[3] in the business management **field**[4].

本書由企業管理領域的權威專家科爾‧瓊斯博士所撰寫。

☐ As you can see, the **cover**[5] of the book is the Earth, which **represents**[6] the Great Mother.

如各位所見，本書的封面是地球，這代表著地球是人類之母。

☐ I choose this textbook because it's not only well-organized but also vividly **illustrated**[7].

我選擇這本教科書是因為它不僅架構嚴謹，而且插圖生動。

☐ This is a useful textbook because it includes discussion questions and activities at the end of each **chapter**[8].

這是一本實用的教科書，因為每章結尾都包含討論問題和活動。

VOCABULARY

① textbook (*n.*) 教科書；課本
② author (*v.*) 撰寫
③ expert (*n.*) 專家
④ field (*n.*) （知識）領域；專業

⑤ cover (*n.*) 封面 (*v.*) 包含
⑥ represent (*v.*) 代表
⑦ illustrated (*adj.*) 有插圖的
⑧ chapter (*n.*) 章節

⊙ TRACK **12**

☐ The most **effective**[9] way to use this textbook is to go through the key vocabulary first and then work through the exercises provided in the back.

使用本教材最有效的方法是先瀏覽關鍵詞彙，再做後面提供的練習題。

☐ You'll need the following two books: *Writing Up* by Marisa Worth and *Academic Way* by Steve Thompson.

各位同學需要準備以下兩本書：瑪麗紗・沃思所寫的《Writing Up》和史蒂夫・湯普森所著的《Academic Way》。

☐ You can find these books at the school bookstore or the **library**[10].

你們可以在學校書店或圖書館找到這些書。

☐ I strongly suggest you take notes since some of the topics I'll discuss aren't in the textbook but will be on the final exam.

我強烈建議同學們要記筆記，因為有些我講到的要點課本中沒提到，但期末會考喔！

☐ You are **encouraged**[11] to **preview**[12] Chapters 2, 5, and 9 before class on Tuesday.

請同學們下週二上課前要先預習第二章、第五章和第九章。

VOCABULARY

⑨ effective (*adj.*) 有效的
⑩ library (*n.*) 圖書館
⑪ encourage (*v.*) 鼓勵
⑫ preview (*v.*) 預習

☐ You'll find readings related to the **lectures**[1] on the class website.

各位可以在我們班網上找到與課程相關的閱讀素材。

☐ Some additional grammar **worksheets**[2] and writing **template**[3] files are available through the learning management system, so please make sure you have access to it.

有些額外的文法學習單和寫作模板文件都可以在我們的學習管理系統中找到,所以請確定你們都有權限可查看。

☐ I'll post three journal articles and five audio recordings on my course page. Please download them after the class.

我將會在我的課程頁面上張貼三篇期刊文章和五個錄音檔。請於課後下載。

☐ Everything on the reading list, including the **reference**[4] books, is available in the library.

在此閱讀清單內的所有資料包括參考書目,都可以在圖書館找到。

☐ PowerPoint files for all my lectures are posted online, so please do go through them before the final exam.

我所有課程的投影片檔案都公佈在網上,請務必在期末考前仔細閱讀。

☐ Let's look at this website together. It has a lot of audio and video files related to language acquisition.

讓我們一起來看這個網站,其中列出了許多關於如何習得語言的音檔和影片。

VOCABULARY

① lecture (*n.*) 講課　　　　　③ template (*n.*) 模板
② worksheet (*n.*) 學習單　　　④ reference (*n.*) 參考

TRACK **13**

☐ I've listed ten AI-related online resources on the second page of the syllabus.

我在課程大綱的第二頁列出了十個 AI 相關的線上資源。

☐ You will be **required**[5] to read at least five journal articles and **summarize**[6] their key points.

同學們要唸至少五篇期刊文獻並做重點摘要。

☐ Please do read all of the assigned materials so you can provide **thoughtful**[7] **contributions**[8] to our class discussions.

請務必讀完所有指派的教材，你才有辦法在課堂討論時提供見解。

☐ Each of you will **complete**[9] an original **research**[10] **project**[11]. But don't worry, I'll provide some **examples**[12] for your reference.

每位同學都要做研究專題。但不用擔心，我會提供範例給你們參考。

Useful Tips

對大學或研究所階段的同學而言，閱讀大量的期刊文獻已是必要的功課。教師可自行指派必讀的文獻，或為了讓同學有練習的機會，也可讓同學在 Google Scholar 網站上使用關鍵字搜尋想讀的期刊。

VOCABULARY

⑤ require (*v.*) 要求
⑥ summarize (*v.*) 概括；總結
⑦ thoughtful (*adj.*) 深思的
⑧ contribution (*n.*) 貢獻

⑨ complete (*v.*) 完成 (*adj.*) 完整的
⑩ research (*n./v.*) 研究
⑪ project (*n.*) 專題
⑫ example (*n.*) 例子

☐ Now, let's turn to the grading **system**[1], which I'm sure everyone wants to know about.

現在，我們來討論大家都想瞭解的成績計算方式。

☐ The **evaluation**[2] criteria are as follows.

同學們的學習評估方式如以下說明。

☐ Your weekly assignments will **account for**[3] 20% of your **grade**[4].

每週的作業將佔成績的百分之二十。

☐ Please note that I also grade all students on exams and class **participation**[5].

請注意，我也將透過考試和課堂參與度來評估同學們的分數。

☐ The midterm exam covers **theory**[6], which is from Unit 2 to Unit 4 in the textbook. The questions will be multiple choice and fill in the blank.

期中考包括理論部分，從課本的第二單元到第四單元。題目為選擇題和填空題。

☐ Some students asked for the questions from **previous**[7] **exams**[8], so I've posted some online for your reference.

有些同學想知道關於考古題的事，所以我在網站上張貼了一些舊題目供大家參考。

VOCABULARY

① system (*n.*) 系統；方法
② evaluation (*n.*) 評估
③ account for 佔……
④ grade (*n.*) 成績
⑤ participation (*n.*) 參與
⑥ theory (*n.*) 理論
⑦ previous (*adj.*) 之前的
⑧ exam (*n.*) 考試 (= examination)

🔊 TRACK **14**

☐ Okay, let's go over the scoring **rubric**[9] for your **oral**[10] presentations.

好的，我們一起看一下口頭報告的評分標準。

☐ Students who answer the last two questions on the worksheet get extra points.

有回答學習單上最後兩道題目的同學可以加分。

☐ This is an open book exam, so you are allowed to **consult**[11] your notes, the textbook, and other reference materials.

這考試允許翻書，因此同學們可以參考手邊的筆記、課本和其他參考資料。

☐ Your essay score will primarily be based on your ability to **organize**[12] and support your ideas.

同學們的論述文評分標準，主要是根據組織和支持意見的能力來給分。

Useful Tips

不少同學會特別注重成績計算方式，或如何取得 A+ 等細節。通常教師會在首堂課中就說明清楚，好讓同學有規則可循，尤其是像 writing 或 speaking 等並非有標準答案，且好壞可能會憑個人觀感而定的項目，便應事前就將 rubrics（評估標準）訂好以求公正。

VOCABULARY

⑨ rubric (*n.*) 說明；提示
⑩ oral (*adj.*) 口語的
⑪ consult (*v.*) 查閱；諮詢
⑫ organize (*v.*) 組織；籌劃

☐ You'll be required to write two essays, which will account for 25% of your total grade.

同學們需要寫兩篇論文,佔總成績的百分之二十五。

☐ The team project is **mandatory**[1], but the book **summary**[2] is **optional**[3].

團體研究專案是一定要做的,但是否寫讀書摘要就由同學自行決定。

☐ Each student needs to give a presentation in English at the end of the semester.

每位同學都要在學期末做一次英文簡報。

☐ To get an A in this course, you need to **attend**[4] all 16 classes and **submit**[5] all the required assignments on time.

本課程要拿到 A 的成績,同學們須參與完整十六堂課並按時繳交要求的作業。

☐ Regarding the research **proposal**[6], please note that I do not give **extensions**[7] after the **due date**[8].

關於研究提案,請注意我不會接受遲交的作業。

VOCABULARY

① mandatory (*adj.*) 強制的
② summary (*n.*) 摘要
③ optional (*adj.*) 可選擇的
④ attend (*v.*) 出席;參與
⑤ submit (*v.*) 送出;提交
⑥ proposal (*n.*) 提案
⑦ extension (*n.*) 延伸;延期;分機
⑧ due date (*n.*) 期限;到期日

⊙ TRACK **15**

☐ For the final team project, please choose a topic, do some research on it, and make a video.

關於最後的團體研究專案，請選擇一個主題，對其進行一些研究並錄製影片。

☐ You will be required to give an individual presentation at the end of the semester.

同學們在學期末時會需要做一場個人簡報。

☐ You must **turn in**[9] your research proposals before the final exam.

同學們都要在期末考之前繳交研究提案。

☐ Please make sure any **devices**[10] you're using for your talk are working before you **present**[11] your research **findings**[12].

在報告研究成果之前，同學們請事先確認任何你會使用到的設備都正常可用。

☐ The essay must be completed by week 10, and please note that I don't take late assignments.

第十週之前要完成論文，並請注意我不收遲交的作業。

<u>VOCABULARY</u>

⑨ turn in 送出
⑩ device (*n.*) 設備
⑪ present (*v.*) 呈現
⑫ finding (*n.*) 調查結果；發現

08

介紹課程使用的線上工具
Introducing Online Tools

☐ We'll be using a variety of online tools in the class.
我們的課程會使用到各種線上工具。

☐ I'm going to show you how the Slido tool should be used.
我來示範給大家看 Slido 工具要如何使用。

☐ Show-Me is a great tool that you can use to **create**[1] presentations and reports.
你要做簡報或報告，Show-Me 是個很棒的工具。

☐ I'll share all class **recordings**[2] on the Dial-In platform.
我會將所有課堂錄音檔都分享在 Dial-In 平台上。

☐ The Read-On app provides you with **various**[3] articles and exercises to improve your reading skills.
這個 Read-On 程式提供了各種文章和練習可讓你增進閱讀技巧。

☐ I'll use Talk-Me to **track**[4] your participation during class.
我會使用 Talk-Me 來檢視大家在課堂上的參與程度。

☐ To access all of the **resources**[5] on the website, you'll need to **register**[6] first.
想要存取此網站上的資源，那要先註冊。

VOCABULARY

① **create** (*v.*) 創造
② **recording** (*n.*) 錄音
③ **various** (*adj.*) 各式的

④ **track** (*v.*) 追蹤
⑤ **resource** (*n.*) 資源
⑥ **register** (*v.*) 登記

⊙ TRACK **16**

☐ This is a tool for online brainstorming. You can use it to interact with other learners.

這是個線上腦力激盪的工具，你可以利用它跟其他學生互動。

☐ I'm going to build a **questionnaire**[7] on i-Ask, and then I'll share the link with you in just a minute.

我要在 i-Ask 平台上建個問卷調查，連結等等就分享給大家。

☐ Now take out your **smartphones**[8] or **tablets**[9] to vote on the questions I just created on Think-Link.

現在請將手機或平板拿出來，到我在 Think-Link 上建立的頁面去投票。

Useful Tips

雖說線上課程的互動性不比實體課程來得直接，但拜科技所賜，不勝枚舉的線上互動工具仍足以讓教師設計出精彩的課程。線上工具種類繁多，教師可依自身的需求 Google 搜尋 online teaching tools 便會出現多種選擇，最重要的還是教師要親自體驗，以檢視介面或功能等是否適合課程使用。

VOCABULARY

⑦ questionnaire (*n.*) 問卷調查
⑧ smartphone (*n.*) 智慧型手機
⑨ tablet (*n.*) 平板電腦

09

☐ I'll be your **instructor**[1]. My name is David Robinson.

我是你們的老師，我叫大衛‧羅賓森。

☐ Hello. I'm teaching this course this semester. Please call me David.

大家好。這學期我會教這門課，請叫我大衛就可以了。

☐ I'm Dr. Robinson, and I've been teaching academic writing courses for more than ten years.

我是羅賓森博士，我教學術寫作課十多年了。

☐ My office is in Jackson Hall, Room 32, which is the last office on the third floor.

我的辦公室是在傑克森館的 32 室，也就是三樓的最後一間。

☐ You can call me at extension 32 for any **urgent**[2] issues, but email is always the best way to reach me.

有任何急事都可以打學校分機 32 找我，但最方便的方式還是透過 email。

☐ My office hours are two to four every Monday and Wednesday afternoon. If you can't make it then, I can meet with you at another time by **appointment**[3].

我的辦公室時間是每週一和週三的下午兩點到四點，假如這時間你們不方便，要約其他時間也歡迎。

VOCABULARY

① instructor (*n.*) 教師
② urgent (*adj.*) 緊急的
③ appointment (*n.*) 約定；約會議

⊡ TRACK **17**

☐ My teaching **philosophy**[4] is that all students are **unique**[5] and each one of you should strive to realize your full **potential**[6].

我的教學理念是，所有同學都是獨特的並且每個人都要試著將潛能全然發揮。

☐ In my class, you will be required to actively **participate**[7] in discussions and contribute your ideas.

在我的課堂上，同學們都要積極地參與討論並貢獻意見。

☐ This is a safe learning **environment**[8], and I want you to take risks and feel free to ask questions and share your thoughts.

教室內是個安全的學習環境，因此我希望同學們勇於嘗試並自在地提問和分享看法。

☐ To **facilitate**[9] learning, I've **incorporated**[10] individual work, team projects, and **hands-on**[11] activities into the syllabus.

為了促進大家學習，我已將個人作業、團隊專案和實作活動整合至課綱內。

○**VOCABULARY**

④ philosophy (*n.*) 理念；哲學
⑤ unique (*adj.*) 獨一無二的
⑥ potential (*n.*) 潛力 (*adj.*) 潛在的
⑦ participate (*v.*) 參與

⑧ environment (*n.*) 環境
⑨ facilitate (*v.*) 促進；協助
⑩ incorporate (*v.*) 併入；加上
⑪ hands-on (*adj.*) 實際動手做的

☐ We've got a couple of new classmates this semester.

這學期我們來了兩位新同學。

☐ Jessica is our new classmate. Let's welcome her.

潔西卡是我們的新同學。讓我們歡迎她。

☐ Sam will be with us from now on. Sam, please tell us a bit about yourself.

從現在開始,山姆會和我們一起學習。山姆,請介紹一下你自己。

☐ Lisa, why don't you start with a **brief**[1] **introduction**[2] of yourself?

麗莎,妳何不先簡單介紹一下妳自己?

☐ Okay, everybody. Please say "Hi" to Gary Hsu, our new classmate here.

好的,各位。請向我們的新同學許凱瑞說聲「嗨」。

☐ Now, I'd like to hear from each of you. Please say your name and what you **expect**[3] to learn from this course.

現在,我想聽聽每個人的介紹。請說出你的姓名以及你希望從本課程中學到什麼。

VOCABULARY

① brief (*adj.*) 簡短的
② introduction (*n.*) 介紹
③ expect (*v.*) 期待

🔘 TRACK **18**

☐ Okay, next we've got Mary Chang. Mary, go ahead please.
好的，接下來是張瑪麗。瑪麗，請開始。

☐ So, Linda, you **mentioned**[4] that you used to work part-time? Would you like to share something about your work experience?
琳達，妳剛說妳之前有打工？妳願意分享一下妳的工作經驗嗎？

☐ We've got two international **students**[5] in the class: Sugi from Indonesia and Soni from India.
我們班上有兩位外籍生：印尼來的蘇吉和印度來的索妮。

☐ Sugi, you go first, okay? Please introduce yourself **briefly**[6] to the class.
蘇吉，你先好嗎？請跟班上同學稍微介紹你自己。

Useful Tips

首堂課同學們大都互不認識，因此教師通常會請學生自我介紹。在台灣的大學內，國際學生也算不少，經過統計大多數來自印度，其次是印尼。當然了，他們在無法使用中文溝通之時，也只能以英語交談。台灣的同學在聆聽國際學生的自我介紹當中，亦可增加使用英文的機會，更可瞭解不同國家的文化。

VOCABULARY

④ mention (*v.*) 提及
⑤ international student 國際學生
⑥ briefly (*adv.*) 精簡地

學生自我介紹
Self-introduction

- [ ] Hello, everyone. My name is Sasuke and I'm from Japan.
  大家好。我的名字是佐助，我來自日本。

- [ ] Good morning. I'm truly **excited**[1] to be here and learn with you guys.
  大家早安。很高興在此和你們一起學習。

- [ ] I just moved to Taipei with my parents last month.
  我上個月剛和父母搬到台北。

- [ ] In my free time I like to read, mostly **fiction**[2].
  我有空就喜歡閱讀，特別是讀小說。

- [ ] I think I'm a pretty **outgoing**[3] person who really enjoys **exchanging**[4] ideas with classmates.
  我自認是個頗外向的人，我非常喜歡與同學交流想法。

- [ ] I've got some work **experience**[5], so I hope I can **contribute**[6] some different **insights**[7] to the **discussions**[8] in the class.
  我有一些工作經驗，所以我希望我能在課堂討論中貢獻一些不同見解。

- [ ] My name is Soni and I'm from India. I'm interested in learning more about Taiwanese history, so here I am.
  我是索妮，我來自印度。我來台灣讀書是因為我對台灣歷史很感興趣。

○ **VOCABULARY** ○

① excited (*adj.*) 興奮的　　　　　　⑤ experience (*n.*) 經驗
② fiction (*n.*) 小說　　　　　　　　⑥ contribute (*v.*) 貢獻
③ outgoing (*adj.*) 開朗的；愛交際的　⑦ insight (*n.*) 見解
④ exchange (*v.*) 交換　　　　　　　⑧ discussion (*n.*) 討論

⊙ TRACK **19**

☐ I used to study engineering, but after studying at City University for a year I found that I'm more interested in business **management**[9]. That's why I changed my major.

我之前是學工程的，但在都市大學上課一年之後，我發覺我對商業管理比較有興趣，因此我就轉系了。

☐ I **joined**[10] a student exchange program and studied in Korea for a year, so I can speak Korean.

我參加過交換學生的計劃，並在韓國上課了一年，因此我會講韓文。

☐ I really like doing **chemistry**[11] **experiments**[12], so I spend a lot of time in the **laboratory**[13].

我很喜歡做化學實驗，我多數時間都待在實驗室內。

Useful Tips

很多人在自我介紹時會突然不知道該說些什麼，此時建議從 "PPF" 角度切入來發想。所謂 PPF 就是：Past / Present / Future，也就是說可以先談及自己「過去」對什麼有興趣，然後帶到「現在」想修習什麼，最後可以聊聊自己對「未來」的目標、期許等。

VOCABULARY

⑨ management (*n.*) 管理
⑩ join (*v.*) 加入；參加
⑪ chemistry (*n.*) 化學
⑫ experiment (*n.*) 實驗
⑬ laboratory (*n.*) 實驗室

☐ I'm looking forward to learning more about academic writing.

我期望學習到更多關於學術寫作方面的知識。

☐ I'm **passionate**[1] about **programming**[2], and that's why I'm taking this course.

我對寫程式充滿熱情,這就是我選這門課程的原因。

☐ I'd like to do more research on how learning foreign languages and brain development are **correlated**[3].

我想做更多關於學習外語和大腦發展之間關聯的研究。

☐ I can't wait to learn more about how **artificial**[4] **intelligence**[5] could **affect**[6] people's lives in the future.

我迫不及待想瞭解更多關於人工智慧如何影響人們未來生活的相關知識。

☐ My **goal**[7] is to get an A in this course, so I know I'll have to work hard on assignments and projects.

我在這門課的目標是成績要拿到 A,所以我知道我必須努力完成作業和專題。

VOCABULARY

① passionate (*adj.*) 有熱情的
② programming (*n.*) 〔電腦〕程式設計
③ correlate (*v.*) 相互關聯
④ artificial (*adj.*) 人造的;假的
⑤ intelligence (*n.*) 智慧;智力
⑥ affect (*v.*) 影響
⑦ goal (*n.*) 目標;終點

🔊 TRACK **20**

☐ I'm really interested in history, and I plan to choose an event in American history as my **term**[8] project.

我對歷史非常感興趣，我打算選研究一個美國歷史事件來當作我的學期專題。

☐ The main reason I'm taking this course is that I want to improve my **critical**[9] analysis skills.

我修習這門課的目的主要是想增進我的批判分析能力。

☐ I really need to **sharpen**[10] my presentation skills, because I think that's a **vital**[11] skill in the workplace.

我真的想要精進我的簡報技巧，因為我認為此能力在職場上至關重要。

☐ I've always had a **keen**[12] interest in **biology**[13] and would really like to **pursue**[14] a career in nursing.

我一直都對生物學有濃厚興趣，並且想要朝醫護界發展職涯。

☐ I'm taking this course because I plan to **apply for**[15] graduate programs in Germany next year.

我選修這堂課是因為我計劃明年要去申請德國的研究所。

VOCABULARY

⑧ term (*n.*) 學期；術語；名稱
⑨ critical (*adj.*) 批判的
⑩ sharpen (*v.*) 加強
⑪ vital (*adj.*) 極其重要的；必不可少的

⑫ keen (*adj.*) 強烈的
⑬ biology (*n.*) 生物學
⑭ pursue (*v.*) 追求
⑮ apply for 申請

Notes

Lectures

講課

複習之前授課內容
Reviewing Previous Lessons

☐ Previously, we discussed some **common**[1] **strategies**[2] that **organizations**[3] use to increase sales.

之前我們討論了企業組織會運用以增加銷售額的常用策略。

☐ What we've been talking about so far is how to think **critically**[4].

到目前為止我們一直在討論的是如何批判性地思考。

☐ In our last class, we were discussing "**positive**[5] **psychology**[6]." Christine, could you please tell us what that is?

上一節課，我們討論了「正向心理學」。克麗絲汀，妳能告訴我們那是什麼嗎？

☐ Last week, we covered choice theory, remember?

上週，我們討論了「選擇理論」的主題，還記得嗎？

☐ When we ended yesterday, we were talking about some unusual animal **behaviors**[7].

昨天課堂結束時，我們正談論某些動物的獨特行為。

☐ All right, last time we looked at some theories, and today we'll start with some **practical**[8] examples.

好的，上次我們看了一些理論，今天我們就從實例開始。

VOCABULARY

① common (*adj.*) 常見的；普遍的
② strategy (*n.*) 策略
③ organization (*n.*) 組織
④ critically (*adv.*) 批判性地

⑤ positive (*adj.*) 正面的；積極的
⑥ psychology (*n.*) 心理學
⑦ behavior (*n.*) 行為
⑧ practical (*adj.*) 實際的

⌾ TRACK **21**

☐ Are you ready for a pop quiz?

你們準備好來個小考了嗎？

☐ Can anyone tell me what **topics**[9] we went over last time? Yes, Cheryl.

有人可以告訴我上次我們討論到什麼主題嗎？雪莉兒，請說。

☐ Okay, let's **review**[10] the PSF **framework**[11]. Does anybody know what PSF **stands for**[12]?

那麼，我們先複習一下 PSF 架構。有同學知道 PSF 全名為何嗎？

☐ On Monday, we talked about **pragmatics**[13]. Josh, please tell us how you would **define**[14] the term.

我們在週一的課討論到「語用學」。喬許，請告訴我們你會如何定義此學科。

Useful Tips

要為同學複習先前的課業內容，傳統方式以透過小考或提問讓同學回答為主；現今網路上可利用的工具頗多，不妨求個變化並增加師生之間的互動性。比方說，Kahoot! 此線上應用程式便是可供教師設計問題並讓學生透過手機回答以增加互動的工具。

VOCABULARY

⑨ topic (*n.*) 主題；話題
⑩ review (*v.*) 複習
⑪ framework (*n.*) 架構

⑫ stand for 代表
⑬ pragmatics (*n.*) 語用學
⑭ define (*v.*) 下定義

☐ Let me show you a great website that has some useful information you will need to complete your assignment.

我要給大家看一個很棒的網站,其中包括你們要完成作業所需要的實用資訊。

☐ Okay, let's start from the Google search page here. Are you with me?

好的,讓我們從 Google 搜尋頁面開始。大家有跟上嗎?

☐ Now, I want you to type the key words "presentation skills" in quotation marks.

現在,我要請你們輸入關鍵詞「演講技巧」。

☐ Right, this is the **database**[1] **portal**[2], and as you can see, the **interface**[3] is pretty user-friendly.

是的,這頁是資料庫入口網頁。如各位所見,其界面相當容易操作。

☐ In the upper left-hand corner, you will see different **categories**[4] of wild animals.

在左上角,你會看到不同類別的野生動物。

☐ Do you all follow me? Now, watch. When I click on this "More Information" icon, it displays a more detailed **description**[5].

大家都有跟上嗎?現在,你們看,在我點擊這個「更多訊息」圖標後,畫面便顯示更多的細節。

VOCABULARY

① database (*n.*)〔電腦〕資料庫;數據庫
② portal (*n.*) 入口
③ interface (*n.*) 界面
④ category (*n.*) 類別
⑤ description (*n.*) 描述

TRACK **22**

☐ If you don't see the icon, please raise your hand, and the teaching **assistant**[6] will help you immediately.

如果沒有找到圖標，請舉手，助教會立即去協助你。

☐ Now, let's learn how to scan a QR code with your smartphones.

現在, 我們來學一下如何使用智慧型手機掃描 QR code。

☐ Please open your **browser**[7] and **type**[8] www.thesaurus.com into the address bar.

請將瀏覽器打開，接著將網址 www.thesaurus.com 打在網址列內。

☐ I need you to download a podcast app first.

我要請大家先下載一個「播客」應用程式。

Useful Tips

在課堂上利用科技軟硬體設備已是必需，為避免同學沒有跟上或是和教師的畫面不同步等狀況，教師應給予清楚明確的指示，並使用 "Are you with me?" 或 "Are you following me?" 等課室用語時常詢問同學的狀況以便提供協助。

○ VOCABULARY
⑥ assistant (*n.*) 助理
⑦ browser (*n.*) 瀏覽器
⑧ type (*v.*) 打字

☐ Well, this video is around 30 minutes, but don't worry, let's only focus on the first three minutes.

這段影片大約三十分鐘，不過別擔心，我們只會聚焦在前三分鐘。

☐ Let's watch this YouTube video together. It's about how artificial intelligence works.

讓我們一起觀看這段有關人工智慧工作原理的 YouTube 影片。

☐ Before I play the film, let me **remind**[1] you that you should pay special **attention**[2] to the part about algorithms, okay?

在我播放影片之前，我想提醒大家，請特別注意演算法部分喔。

☐ In this video, the speaker will be talking about the **definition**[3] of success. I want you guys to take notes and see if you agree with the speaker.

在此影片中，講者將談論成功的定義。我希望你們做些筆記，並想看看你是否同意該講者的觀點。

☐ Please pay attention to what the speaker says, **jot down**[4] some key points, and I'll ask you to share what you noticed with your partners.

請注意聽講者所說的話，記下一些要點，我會請你與同學分享看法。

VOCABULARY

① remind (*v.*) 提醒
② attention (*n.*) 注意力

③ definition (*n.*) 定義
④ jot down 記下

⊡ TRACK **23**

☐ All right, after watching this video, I want you to talk about what **impressed**[5] you the most.

好的，看完這段影片，我想請同學講一個讓你印象最深刻的點。

☐ **Transcripts**[6] of all videos are available in our Google Classroom.

所有影片的講稿都可在我們班的 Google Classroom 頁面上找到。

☐ We're going to watch this short video twice, so don't worry if you miss some information the first time.

我們會看此短片兩次，所以假如第一次錯過一些資訊也不用擔心。

☐ Okay, today we're going to talk about a new **concept**[7]: YouTube video essays. Does anyone know anything about this genre?

那麼，我們今天要來討論一個新概念，也就是 YouTube 影像論文。有任何人知道這類的影片嗎？

☐ I want each group to produce a short video **introducing**[8] the product you just designed.

我想請每組錄一段短片來介紹你們剛才所設計的產品。

Useful Tips

在課堂上搭配播放的影片不宜過長，一般來說大約花五分鐘左右來解說一概念，同學的接受度較高；若是數十分鐘或一小時的完整影片，可以請同學在課前先預習，如此在課堂中方可更有效率地討論。

VOCABULARY

⑤ impress (*v.*) 使印象深刻；使感動
⑥ transcript (*n.*) 錄音稿；逐字稿

⑦ concept (*n.*) 概念
⑧ introduce (*v.*) 介紹

☐ To begin with, let's do a quick **warm-up**[1] **activity**[2].
讓我們很快做個暖身活動來開始今天的課程。

☐ I'd like to start today's class with a **pop quiz**[3].
我想在今天課程的開始來個小考。

☐ I hope you all did your **homework**[4]. Let's begin with the review questions.
希望大家都有做功課。讓我們從複習一些問題開始。

☐ Let's begin by reviewing what we covered last night.
我們先來複習昨晚所討論過的內容。

☐ Now let's do an activity I designed to improve your reading skills.
我設計了個活動以增進同學們的閱讀技巧,現在就來進行吧。

☐ This is a group discussion activity, so I'm going to **divide**[5] you into groups.
這是小組討論活動,所以我要將同學們分成幾個小組。

○ VOCABULARY
① warm-up (*n.*) 熱身;準備
② activity (*n.*) 活動
③ pop quiz 隨堂測驗
④ homework (*n.*) 回家功課
⑤ divide (*v.*) (使) 分開;(使) 分組

◯ TRACK **24**

☐ I hope you are all ready for this exciting activity.

我希望你們都準備好要開始這個有趣的活動了。

☐ Are you all clear about what to do? Do you want me to go over the **instructions**[6] again?

你們都清楚要做什麼嗎？需要我將規則再講一次嗎？

☐ This is a **communication**[7] activity, so I want you to work **in pairs**[8].

這是個關於溝通的活動，因此我要你們兩兩一組。

☐ Let's listen to a **conversation**[9] first. Please pay careful attention to what the woman says.

我們先來聽段對話。請特別注意女子說些什麼。

Useful Tips

雙語教育／英語授課的精髓之一便是要「創造讓同學使用英語溝通的機會」，而要達到此目的，教師須設計各式可分組討論、共同發想點子的活動。通常在活動開始之前，應先說明活動的目的與規則等事項，以使同學瞭解任務並達到學習效果。

VOCABULARY

⑥ instruction (*n.*) 指示
⑦ communication (*n.*) 溝通
⑧ in pairs 成對地
⑨ conversation (*n.*) 對話；談話

☐ We need five teams for this activity, so let's **form**[1] teams of three.

此活動需要五個小隊，那就請三人一組。

☐ Please **split**[2] into two groups, so you should have five **members**[3] in a group.

請分成兩個小組，所以應該有五個人在一個小組中。

☐ Let's form two teams. So, Jessie, Linda, and Alex, you three are Team A. And Vivian, Chris, and Paul, you three are Team B, okay?

讓我們來分兩隊。潔希、琳達、艾力克斯，你們三個在 A 組，薇薇安、克里斯、保羅，你們三個在 B 組，可以嗎？

☐ What I want you to do first is to come up with a name for your team, please.

我想先請你們幫團隊取一個名字。

☐ Please find a **partner**[4] first, and then I'm going to **assign**[5] you some discussion questions.

請先找個搭擋，我隨後會分配給你們一些討論問題。

☐ I'm going to use the system to assign you guys to different groups **randomly**[6].

我會用系統將你們隨機分配到不同的組中。

VOCABULARY

① form (v.)（使）形成
② split (v.)（使）分開
③ member (n.) 成員；會員

④ partner (n.) 夥伴；同伴
⑤ assign (v.) 分配；指派
⑥ randomly (adv.) 隨機地

⏺ TRACK **25**

☐ Please **nominate**[7] a team leader first.

請先指派一位組長。

☐ All right, now you have ten minutes to discuss the questions on the worksheet.

好的，現在你們有十分鐘的時間來討論學習單上的問題。

☐ Sean, can you work with Mark, please?

尚恩，你可以跟馬克一組嗎？謝謝。

在實體課程教室

☐ We need to **rearrange**[8] the desks today for this **special**[9] activity.

我們今天要做個特別的活動，因此要重排一下桌子。

Useful Tips

教師幫同學分組做活動的方式應依照活動的類型或時間等因素來變化。有些活動適合個別單獨做，如此每位同學便有 100% 的練習機會；有些兩人一組的活動，雖說看似每人練習的機會為 50%，但其實透過兩人互動也練習到了溝通的技巧。

VOCABULARY

⑦ nominate (*v.*) 任命；提名
⑧ rearrange (*v.*) 重新安排
⑨ special (*adj.*) 特別的

06 講解規則
Stating Rules

☐ Now, let me tell you the rules for this activity. Please pay attention.

現在我來跟大家說明這個活動的規則。請注意聽。

☐ The rules are easy. First of all, you guys pick a business problem from the list and then brainstorm ideas to **solve**[1] the problem.

規則很簡單。首先,你們從列表中選出一個商業問題,然後,集思廣益想出可解決此問題的點子。

☐ There are some simple rules you have to **stick to**[2].

有一些簡單的規則請務必遵守。

☐ What I want you guys to do now is read the **passage**[3] on the worksheet and summarize the three key points.

現在我要你們做的是閱讀學習單上的短文並歸納出三個要點。

☐ The first thing you need to do is to choose a topic. After that, you should search for **relevant**[4] information on the Internet.

第一個步驟是選擇一個主題。然後,在網路上搜集相關資料。

☐ Your task is to produce a **poster**[5] that **promotes**[6] the new product you just designed.

你們的任務是製作一張海報來宣傳你們剛剛設計的新產品。

VOCABULARY

① solve (*v.*) 解決
② stick to 遵守;堅持
③ passage (*n.*) 短文

④ relevant (*adj.*) 相關的
⑤ poster (*n.*) 海報
⑥ promote (*v.*) 宣傳

TRACK **26**

☐ I want to make sure you all understand the tasks.

我想確認一下你們都瞭解要做什麼任務。

☐ Okay, now please read the short passage **silently**[7] first and **underline**[8] the vocabulary that you don't understand.

好的，現在請先默唸此短文，並將不認識的單字劃起來。

☐ I'll share the instructions on my screen and let's go through everything together.

我會將規則分享在螢幕上，讓我們一起看過一次。

在實體課程教室

☐ Please take a worksheet and pass the rest to the person sitting behind you.

請每人拿一張學習單並將多的傳到後面。

Useful Tips

向同學講解活動時最重要的是要清楚易懂，並明確地點出要完成的步驟。解說步驟時，可多利用指示性的字詞，例如 first ...、second ...、next ...、following that ...、after that ...、finally ... 等，來讓同學知道步驟的先後順序。

VOCABULARY

⑦ silently (*adv.*) 默默地
⑧ underline (*v.*) 劃底線

確認同學們都準備好了

Making Sure Everyone's Ready

☐ Do you all understand the **rules**[1]?

你們都瞭解規則嗎？

☐ Are you all **ready**[2]?

大家都準備好了嗎？

☐ Is everything clear now?

現在一切都清楚嗎？

☐ Shall we begin?

我們可以開始了嗎？

☐ If you have any questions, raise your hand.

如果還有任何問題，請舉手。

☐ Ready? Let's go.

準備好了？開始吧。

○ **VOCABULARY**
① rule (*n.*) 規則
② ready (*adj.*) 準備好的

◉ TRACK **27**

☐ Are you all following me?
同學們都有跟上嗎？

☐ Before you begin, any questions?
開始之前還有沒有任何問題？

☐ I've posted the instructions in the **chat**³ window.
我已將規則都貼在「聊天區」了。

在實體課程教室

☐ I've written the instructions on the board.
我已將規則都寫在黑／白板上了。

Useful Tips

確認同學是否瞭解活動步驟的課室英語，常用的幾句熟練之後便可隨時派上用場，例如 "Do you all understand?" 或 "Are you ready?" 等都很實用，而若是擔心同學有其他疑慮，還可加上一句 "Any questions?"。

VOCABULARY

③ chat (*n.*) 閒聊

☐ All right, Jessie. Good job. So, who's next?

很好，潔希。做得好。那麼，下一個換誰？

☐ Who would like to say something about this picture?

誰要來描述一下這張照片？

☐ Now, Will. It's your turn, please.

現在，威爾。輪到你了，請吧。

☐ Come on, any **volunteers**[1]?

來吧，有人自願嗎？

☐ Let's invite Robert to voice his **opinions**[2].

讓我們邀請羅伯來發表一下看法。

☐ Whose turn is it now?

現在輪到誰了？

☐ Tiffany, would you like to share your **thoughts**[3]?

蒂芬妮，妳想分享妳的想法嗎？

☐ Jason, how about you? What do you think?

傑森，那你呢？你認為怎樣？

VOCABULARY

① volunteer (*n.*) 自願者
② opinion (*n.*) 意見
③ thought (*n.*) 想法

在實體課程教室

☐ Let's start with Team A. Members please come to the front.

我們就從 A 組開始。成員請到前面來。

☐ Lisa, please **explain**[4] the **rationale**[5] behind your decision, okay?

麗莎,請解釋一下妳是根據什麼原因來下此決定的呢?

Useful Tips

做完討論活動之後,教師通常會請同學發表討論結果與看法等,若僅是問 "Any volunteers?" 請同學自願發表的話,通常結果就是一片安靜。要解決這樣的問題、讓學生提振精神,教師不妨直接點名或請每人輪流發表,亦或採取些製造緊張感的小撇步,例如丟骰子擲號碼叫學號,或用電腦隨機抽籤等都是不錯的方式。

○ VOCABULARY

④ explain (*v.*) 解釋
⑤ rationale (*n.*) 原理;根本原因

☐ Try to come up with two more ideas. I'm sure you can do it.

請嘗試再多想出兩個點子。我相信你可以做得到。

☐ You guys have already finished? Okay, I suggest that you exchange **roles**[1] and **practice**[2] the set again.

你們完成了嗎？我建議你們互換角色，根據這套題組再練一遍。

☐ Use the worksheet and write down as many ideas as you can think of on the **chart**[3].

請看學習單並在此處的圖表中盡可能多地寫下你能想到的點子。

☐ Okay, now **analyze**[4] the problem from different **perspectives**[5].

好的，現在你可以從不同的角度分析這個問題。

☐ Keep talking to each other. You've still got time.

繼續討論。你們還有點時間。

☐ Wow, you guys have already come up with a solution. Good job. Now, list the **pros and cons**[6] of the solution, okay?

哇，你們已經想出了解決方案。好棒。現在，請試著列出此解決方案的利與弊。

☐ What else? Keep brainstorming more ideas, please.

還有呢？請繼續發想更多點子。

VOCABULARY

① role (*n.*) 角色
② practice (*v.*) 練習
③ chart (*n.*) 圖表

④ analyze (*v.*) 分析
⑤ perspective (*n.*) 觀點；看法
⑥ pros and cons 優缺點

◉ TRACK **29**

☐ Let me give you a **hint**[7]. The country is **famous**[8] for its **abundant**[9] natural resources.

我給你們一點線索。那國家以豐富的天然資源聞名。

☐ You should find more relevant **facts**[10] to support your **argument**[11], right? Okay, keep thinking. You can do it.

你應該找更多相關事證來支持你的論點，沒錯吧？那麼，就繼續想吧。你可以的。

☐ Have you taken all the **details**[12] into consideration? No? Well, keep working on it.

你們有將所有的細節都考慮進去了嗎？沒有？那麼，就繼續做吧。

Useful Tips

在分組討論時，同學可能會遇到瓶頸而無法接續討論的狀況，這時與其直接公佈答案，倒不如持續鼓勵學生再多思考並給予協助。別忘了也要適時地給予正面的鼓勵話語：Try again. I believe you can do it. 「再試一次，我相信你做得到」！

VOCABULARY

⑦ hint (*n.*) 暗示
⑧ famous (*adj.*) 有名的
⑨ abundant (*adj.*) 豐富的

⑩ fact (*n.*) 事實；實際情況
⑪ argument (*n.*) 論點
⑫ detail (*n.*) 細節

☐ What kind of information do you want to include in your presentation?

你們想要在簡報中包括哪一類資訊？

☐ Your aim is to design an **advertisement**[1] for a new product, so you should **consider**[2] how to **attract**[3] the attention of potential customers.

你的目標是要設計一個展示新產品的廣告，所以你應該考慮的是如何吸引潛在顧客的注意力。

☐ Work with your team members and try to brainstorm as many ideas as **possible**[4] first.

跟你的團隊成員一起作業，首先請試著集思廣益盡可能想多些點子。

☐ You should decide the main **theme**[5] of your story instead of just jumping right into the details.

你們應該先決定故事的主題，而不是太快地切入細節。

☐ What are the three most important points you'd like to present?

你們想呈現的三個最重要的論點是什麼？

☐ For now, please focus on two **elements**[6] to include in your experiment.

現在，請聚焦在你們的實驗中想要包括哪兩個元素。

VOCABULARY

① advertisement (*n.*) 廣告
② consider (*v.*) 考慮；認為
③ attract (*v.*) 吸引

④ possible (*adj.*) 可能的
⑤ theme (*n.*) 主題
⑥ element (*n.*) 要素；部分

⊙ TRACK **30**

☐ It seems to me that you've **overlooked**[7] some important considerations. Paul, what other details should be taken into account?

在我看來你忽略掉一些重要的細節了。保羅，還有什麼細節應納入考慮？

☐ What opinion is the speaker presenting? Think more about that, okay?

這講者所提的論點為何？可以朝這方面思考。

☐ The claim "many students agreed" is not very precise. What **percentage**[8] of the students agreed?

「很多學生都同意」這說法不是很精確。是有多少比例的學生同意呢？

☐ That's a good idea, but try to be more **specific**[9], okay? What information do you have to include in order to help your **audience**[10] understand better?

那點子不錯，但請試著更明確點，好嗎？為了幫助聽眾更容易瞭解，你必須加入什麼內容？

Useful Tips

做課堂討論活動時，教師適時地給予建議、線索更可協助學生完成任務。此時與其用指令句（例如 You can just do ...），倒不如善加利用疑問句，讓學生自行想答案與找方向成效更佳，比方說 What if ...? 或 Do you think ...? 等皆可引導同學繼續從不同角度思考。

°VOCABULARY

⑦ overlook (*v.*) 忽視；忽略
⑧ percentage (*n.*) 比例

⑨ specific (*adj.*) 明確的
⑩ audience (*n.*) 閱聽眾

☐ William, would you please share your screen, so everybody can see the poster you designed?

威廉，能不能分享一下你的螢幕，讓大家都能看到你剛設計的海報？

☐ I'll give you guys five more minutes to upload your presentation files to Google Classroom.

我再給大家五分鐘的時間將你們的簡報檔案上傳到我們的 Google Classroom 專頁。

☐ Now, what I want you to do is upload your writing assignments to our shared homework folder.

現在，我要請你們將寫作作業上傳到我們共享的「功課」資料夾。

☐ All right, now William, please show us the solutions you've come up with, okay?

好的，威廉，請展示給大家看你們那組所討論出的解決方案。

☐ All five team leaders, please upload the videos you've made to the public folder.

五組的組長，請將你們做的影片上傳到公用資料夾內。

☐ Wow, Carol, you listed so many ideas. Could you please group them into sections?

哇，卡蘿，妳列出好多意見耶。妳可以將這些點子分類嗎？

☐ Now, let's take a look at what **adjectives**[1] you've used to **describe**[2] the **landscapes**[3] of Taiwan.

現在我們就來看看你們用了什麼形容詞來描述台灣的景象。

> 在實體課程教室

☐ All right. Now, Team One, please **stick**[4] the advertisement you just designed on the wall.

好的。現在，第一組，請把你們剛剛設計的廣告貼在牆上。

☐ Will the leader of each team please come up here and put your **illustration**[5] on the whiteboard.

請各組長上來，將你們的插圖貼在白板上。

☐ Team Two, once you're ready, please come to the **stage**[6] and present your findings.

第二組，你們準備好，就請上台報告你們那組的發現。

Useful Tips

做完課堂活動之後，最重要的是評估成效，看同學是否有產出預期的學習成果。以線上課程而言，可將學生作品（音檔、簡報、貼文……等）公佈在共享的雲端工具（例如 Padlet）上，讓學生們互相參考學習。

VOCABULARY

① adjective (*n.*) 形容詞
② describe (*v.*) 描述
③ landscape (*n.*) 風景；景色

④ stick (*v.*) 釘住；黏貼固定住
⑤ illustration (*n.*) 插圖；圖示
⑥ stage (*n.*) 舞台；講台

☐ Wow, all five groups have completed your experiments. **Wonderful**[1] job.

哇，五組都完成了實驗。做得真好。

☐ James, please share with us what you've learned from this activity.

詹姆士，請與我們分享你從這次活動中學到了什麼。

☐ Now, after working with your classmates on this project, how do you feel?

現在，與同學合作完成這個專題後，你感覺如何？

☐ All right, after this exercise, you should now understand that effective communication also **involves**[2] body language.

好的，做完這個練習，你現在應該明白有效的溝通也包括肢體語言。

☐ Okay, you've done an **excellent**[3] job. Let's give ourselves a big hand!

好的，你們做得很棒。我們給自己鼓勵鼓勵吧！

○ **VOCABULARY** ○

① wonderful (*adj.*) 很棒的
② involve (*v.*) 牽涉
③ excellent (*adj.*) 傑出的

⦿ TRACK **32**

更多肯定的說法

☐ A round of **applause**[4] for all of the students. You did a great job.
讓我們為所有同學鼓掌。你們表現得非常出色。

☐ Wonderful job, everybody. You all put in the time and completed all of the assigned tasks.
每個人都做得太棒了。你們都花了很多時間來完成指派的作業。

☐ You have all made a lot of **progress**[5]. Well done!
你們都進步相當多。做得很棒!

☐ I'm really impressed with your performance. Good job!
我對你們的表現感到驚豔,做得好!

☐ Everyone in the class has been working hard, and it shows.
班上每位同學都很努力,老師看得出來。

Useful Tips

不論同學的實作成果如何,全心投入的學習精神都是值得嘉許的,因此在總結活動的成果之後,別忘了對學生說聲 "You did a great job." 給予真心鼓勵喔!

VOCABULARY

④ applause (*n.*) 拍手;鼓掌
⑤ progress (*n.*) 進步;進展

Notes

Assessments

評量

T So, what's the best solution to this problem then? Anyone? Yes, Jessie.

那麼，這個問題的最佳解決方案是什麼？有人有想法嗎？是，潔希。

S Well, I think the company should **expand**[1] internationally.

嗯，我認為該公司應擴展國際市場。

T John, can you share with us one way to **protect**[2] the **environment**[3]?

約翰，你能和我們分享一下如何保護環境嗎？

S Um, people should definitely stop burning coal and oil.

嗯，人們絕對應停止燒煤和石油。

T Which of these problems would you find most challenging?

你覺得這些問題中哪一項最具挑戰性？

S Well, in this case, the biggest challenge is developing new products that **meet**[4] the needs of the business's current customers.

在此案例中，最具挑戰性的問題是開發新產品以滿足該企業既有客戶的需求。

VOCABULARY

① expand (*v.*) 拓展
② protect (*v.*) 保護
③ environment (*n.*) 環境
④ meet (*v.*) 達到

🔘 TRACK **33**

T Which **option**[5] do you think is better: **hiring**[6] more **employees**[7] or asking **current**[8] employees to **work overtime**[9]?

你認為哪個選項比較好：雇用更多員工，或是要求現有員工加班？

S The company should definitely **recruit**[10] more workers.

公司的確是應招聘更多員工。

T I want you to think about how to solve the problem of traffic **congestion**[11].

我想請你們想想看如何解決交通壅塞的問題。

S The government should encourage people to **carpool**[12].

政府應鼓勵人們共乘。

T What's the root **cause**[13] of the problem? Talk it over with your partners.

問題的根本原因是什麼？跟你們的搭檔討論一下。

S Okay, so we should **determine**[14] what happened and why it happened, right?

好的，所以我們應確認發生了什麼事以及這事為什麼會發生，對嗎？

VOCABULARY

⑤ option (*n.*) 選項
⑥ hire (*v.*) 雇用
⑦ employee (*n.*) 雇員
⑧ current (*adj.*) 目前的
⑨ work overtime 加班

⑩ recruit (*v.*) 雇用
⑪ congestion (*n.*) 壅塞
⑫ carpool (*v.*) 共乘
⑬ cause (*n.*) 起因
⑭ determine (*v.*) 查明

T Joe, if you were in such a **situation**[15], what would you do?

喬，要是你遇到此狀況，你會怎麼辦？

S Well, I would consult my **supervisor**[16] immediately.

我會馬上詢問主管的意見。

T Linda, can you explain why the business strategy works?

琳達，妳可以解釋一下為何此商業策略會成功嗎？

S Yes. It works because the company focuses on meeting customers' needs.

好的。之所以會成功是因為該公司極力滿足客戶的需求。

T What research **methods**[17] would you use to find an answer to the question, Jack?

你會用什麼研究方法來尋找此問題的答案，傑克？

S I would conduct **surveys**[18] and interviews to collect data.

我會用問卷和面談的方式來收集資料。

T What's one way to think about a very complicated situation like this one? Anyone?

像這樣極複雜的情況該如何思考？有人可回答嗎？

S Well, I would step back and look at the problem from a bird's eye view.

我會退一步用比較宏觀的角度來看問題。

VOCABULARY

⑮ situation (*n.*) 情況；處境
⑯ supervisor (*n.*) 管理者
⑰ method (*n.*) 方法
⑱ survey (*n.*) 調查

⊙ TRACK **35**

T → **Teacher**　　**S** → **Student**

S Well, our team members all think that option A is the best.

我們的團隊成員都認為選項 A 是最好的。

T Okay, but I'm afraid you've **ignored**[1] the **possibility**[2] that children's behavior might change. Do you want to think about it some more?

好的，但恐怕你們忽略了兒童行為可能會改變的可能性。你們要不要再想一想？

S Can I **assume**[3] that once the company expands its business abroad, sales **revenue**[4] will **increase**[5]?

我可以假設說一旦公司把業務拓展到國外，他們的銷售收入會增加嗎？

T It's possible. But now I want you to ask yourself: what's the **root cause**[6] of the company's problem?

有可能。但現在我想請你問問自己：這公司問題的根本起因是什麼？

S Young people become **addicted**[7] to playing online games because they have too much **freedom**[8].

年輕人沉溺於玩線上遊戲，因為他們有太多的自由。

T That's an interesting point, Jesse. Can you please **elaborate**[9] on that?

這是一個有趣的想法，傑西。你能更詳細說明一下嗎？

S I think that children should learn foreign languages as early as possible.

我認為孩子應儘早學習外語。

T All right. I want to hear from someone who is against this idea. Anyone?

好。我想聽聽反對這個想法的人的意見。有誰要分享？

S People should plant more trees in order to save the earth.

為了拯救地球，人們應該多種點樹。

T Great idea, Derrick. What other actions can people take to protect the environment? Keep thinking.

好主意，德瑞克。人們還可以採取哪些其他行動來保護環境？請繼續思考。

S We've come up with two solutions to the problem.

我們為這個問題想出了兩種解決方案。

T Good job. Now I want you guys to **evaluate**[10] the pros and cons of the two solutions, okay?

做得好。現在我想請你們評估那兩種解決方案的優缺點，OK 嗎？

S Well, this is a **complex**[11] problem.

這問題真的很複雜。

T It is, but you could try to **diagram**[12] all of the **factors**[13]. **Visuals**[14] can be helpful in problem solving.

是很複雜，但你可以試著將其中的要素用圖形表示。視覺資料對解決問題頗有幫助。

S This is the product we designed.

這是我們設計的產品。

T Okay, good. I'd like to hear how you did it.

很好。我想聽看看你們是怎麼做的。

S Many factors might **influence**[15] children's learning **outcomes**[16].

很多因素都會影響到孩子的學習成果。

T Good point, Grace. Can you provide some examples?

有道理，葛瑞絲。妳可以舉些例子嗎？

S This article **indicates**[17] that it's easier to **raise**[18] children now than in the past.

這篇文章指出現在教養小孩比過去簡單耶。

T Do you agree? Think about it and tell me why or why not.

你同意嗎？想想看並告訴我理由。

VOCABULARY

① ignore (v.) 忽略
② possibility (n.) 可能性
③ assume (v.) 假定
④ revenue (n.) 營收
⑤ increase (v.) 增加
⑥ root cause 根本起因
⑦ addicted (adj.) 上癮的
⑧ freedom (n.) 自由
⑨ elaborate (v.) 詳加說明
⑩ evaluate (v.) 評估
⑪ complex (adj.) 複雜的
⑫ diagram (v.) 圖示
⑬ factor (n.) 因素；要素
⑭ visuals (n.) 視覺素材
⑮ influence (v.) 影響
⑯ outcome (n.) 結果
⑰ indicate (v.) 指出；表明
⑱ raise (v.) 養育

03 引導更多點子
Eliciting More Ideas

S In this passage, it says that in order to **succeed**[1], we should **behave**[2] more like the people around us.

在這段文章中，它說為了成功，我們應該學別人耶。

T Well, is the **statement**[3] **convincing**[4]? What do you think?

嗯，這個說法有說服力嗎？你認為如何？

S The company decided to **withdraw**[5] from the Thai market.

該公司決定退出泰國市場。

T Yes, Jack. Thank you for reading the sentence. Can anyone explain the reason behind that? Linda, want to try?

是的，傑克。謝謝你唸這句。有人可以解釋這事背後的原因嗎？琳達，想試試嗎？

S The story **implies**[6] that talking to strangers is not a wise choice.

這個故事暗示與陌生人交談並不是一個明智的決定。

T All right. So, if you were in such a situation, what would you do, Paul?

好。那麼，如果你處於這種情況，你會怎麼做，保羅？

VOCABULARY

① succeed (*v.*) 成功
② behave (*v.*) 表現
③ statement (*n.*) 陳述；說法
④ convincing (*adj.*) 有說服力的
⑤ withdraw (*v.*) 撤出
⑥ imply (*v.*) 暗喻

S Well, I don't think what Jack just said is **reasonable**[7].

我不認為傑克剛才說的有道理耶。

T Oh? So, Mary, you don't agree with Jack. Can you tell us why?

哦？瑪麗，所以妳不同意傑克囉。妳能告訴我們為什麼嗎？

S The Internet makes people's lives a lot more **convenient**[8].

網路為人們帶來便利的生活。

T Okay, Jessie. Now can you think of any **disadvantages**[9] of the Internet?

好的，潔希。那妳能想到網路的任何缺點嗎？

S I'm not sure if this is a fact or an opinion.

我不確定這是「事實」還是「觀點」。

T Tell me first, Kyle, how do you explain the **difference**[10] between facts and opinions?

首先請告訴我，凱爾，你如何解釋「事實」和「觀點」之間的區別？

VOCABULARY

⑦ reasonable (*adj.*) 合理的

⑧ convenient (*adj.*) 方便的

⑨ disadvantage (*n.*) 缺點

⑩ difference (*n.*) 差異

S I don't think the Internet has made people's lives easier.

我不認為網路讓人們的生活更便利了。

T Well, why not? Tell me more.

為什麼？再多說一些。

S Uh ... the company is using ... uh ... a strategy ...

呃……那公司是用……呃……策略……

T Remember the **case**[11] we analyzed yesterday? What was the strategy that the company used?

記得我們昨天分析的案例嗎？那公司採取了什麼策略？

S I think this project is really difficult and I don't know where to start.

我覺得這個專題太難做了，我不知道從哪裡開始。

T All right, Tim. Tell me what problems you've **encountered**[12].

好的，提姆。跟我講你遇到什麼困難。

S This chapter is about the "80/20 Rule".

這章節是在討論「八十／二十法則」。

T Yes, so what's another name for the "80/20 Rule"? Anyone?

是的，「八十／二十法則」還有另一個說法。有誰知道？

VOCABULARY
⑪ case (*n.*) 案例
⑫ encounter (*v.*) 遭遇

Responding to Students' Answers

T → **Teacher**   S → **Student**

S We've decided to form a study group and help each other **prepare**[1] for the exams.

我們決定組一個讀書會，互相幫助為考試做準備。

T That's a wonderful idea.

這是個好主意。

S Well, I consider some of the subject-verb agreement rules rather **confusing**[2].

我認為有些「主動詞一致」的規則有些難懂。

T Don't worry. As long as you keep practicing, they'll start to **make sense**[3].

別擔心。只要持續練習，這些規則就會變得有跡可循。

S I'm thinking about a career in data science. I'm especially interested in **statistics**[4].

我正在考慮從事數據科學的職業。我對統計學特別感興趣。

T I'm certain it shouldn't be a problem for you.

我確信這對你來說應不是問題。

VOCABULARY

① prepare (*v.*) 準備
② confusing (*adj.*) 令人困惑的
③ make sense 有道理；具意義
④ statistics (*n.*) 統計資料；統計學

S Explaining information to other classmates actually helps **reinforce**[5] my **mastery**[6] of the information.

解釋資訊給其他同學聽讓我自己對資訊更加瞭解了。

T Yes, you're exactly right, Rose.

的確，妳說得對，蘿絲。

S A good leader should develop problem-solving skills and be able to analyze issues from different perspectives.

一個好的領導者應培養解決問題的能力，並能夠從不同的角度分析問題。

T Wow, I like your answer, Tony.

哇，我喜歡你的回答，湯尼。

S Chapter 4 has a **massive**[7] amount of detail.

第四章涵蓋了非常多細節。

T That's true. But if you read it carefully, you won't find it too difficult to understand the main points.

是的。但如果你仔細閱讀，你會發現其中的要點並不是太難懂。

S I've designed an AI system that can **identify**[8] human **emotions**[9].

我設計了一套可偵測人類情緒的 AI 系統。

T That's quite **amazing**[10], Charlie.

真的好厲害，查里。

VOCABULARY

⑤ reinforce (*v.*) 加強
⑥ mastery (*n.*) 精通
⑦ massive (*adj.*) 大量的
⑧ identify (*v.*) 識別
⑨ emotion (*n.*) 情緒
⑩ amazing (*adj.*) 非常好的

S I'm interested in conducting research on animal communication.

我對做動物溝通的研究有興趣。

T Great. Where do you plan to start?

很棒。你打算從什麼開始做？

S Mrs. Chen, I don't quite understand some of the concepts you covered today.

陳老師，您今天談到的有些概念我不是很瞭解。

T Okay, which areas **in particular**[11] need further **explanation**[12], Andy?

好的，跟我講哪些地方特別需要多加解釋，安迪？

S **Professor**[13], I'm confused about the difference between the two theories you discussed in your talk.

教授，我對您談論的這兩個理論的差異有些混淆。

T Let me try to **clarify**[14].

我來替你解惑。

VOCABULARY

⑪ in particular 特別；尤其
⑫ explanation (*n.*) 解釋
⑬ professor (*n.*) 教授
⑭ clarify (*v.*) 闡明

05

指派作業
Assigning Homework

T I want you to finish reading Unit 5 before the next class.

我希望你們在下一堂課之前讀完第五單元。

S Should we also read the "Case **Analysis**[1]" part?

我們也要看「案例分析」部分嗎？

T Please answer all ten questions on pages 45 and 46.

請回答第 45 和 46 頁上的十個問題。

S When is the **deadline**[2] for this assignment?

這項功課的截止日期是什麼時候？

T What you should do first is choose a topic for your term project.

你應該先選個主題當學期專題。

S Can I talk to you about my topic after class?

課後我可以和您討論一下我的主題嗎？

VOCABULARY

① analysis (*n.*) 分析
② deadline (*n.*) 截止日

⊙ TRACK **41**

T The assignment for the next class is to write a story with a **surprising**[3] **ending**[4].

下一堂課的作業是寫一個結局出乎意料的故事。

S Wow, I think this is going to be fun.

哇，我覺得這會很有趣。

T Please read Chapter 2 and identify the author's three main points.

請閱讀第二章並找出作者的三個要點。

S Should we submit a **report**[5]?

我們要交報告嗎？

T What I'd like you to do is design a new product and make a presentation to promote it.

我希望你們做的是設計一個新產品並做簡報推廣它。

S Is this an **individual**[6] assignment or a team project?

這是個人作業還是小組專案？

VOCABULARY

③ surprising (*adj.*) 令人驚訝的
④ ending (*n.*) 結尾

⑤ report (*n.*) 報告
⑥ individual (*adj.*) 個人的

T Please complete this chart and upload it to our shared folder by this Friday.

請完成這張表格，並在週五前上傳到共享資料夾內。

S I think some of us may need more time to do it.

我們有些人可能需要多一點時間。

T I want you to **produce**[7] an online **portfolio**[8] of your work.

我想要你做一個線上作品集。

S Okay, but who is the intended audience?

好的，但目標聽眾是誰呢？

T Tom, what have you been doing recently?

湯姆，你最近都忙些什麼呢？

S I've just been thinking about my next research project.

我一直在想下個研究專案的事。

T I want you to visit a gallery and write a site visit report.

我要你們去參觀一間美術館並寫一份實地參訪報告。

S Do you have any particular **guidelines**[9] you want us to follow in the report?

報告有特別須遵守的書寫規則嗎？

VOCABULARY

⑦ produce (*v.*) 製造；產出
⑧ portfolio (*n.*) 作品集
⑨ guideline (*n.*) 方針；準則

要確認學生對所教過的知識是否理解，最直接的方式之一便是提問並讓同學描述一次所習得之內容。在問題的設計方面，建議可參考 Bloom's Taxonomy 架構，除了 remember 與 understand 類的題目，也應多提出 apply、analyze、evaluate 與 create 等面向之問題，以刺激學生的思考力。

雖說教師應尊重學生的差異與意願，但面對個性內斂、較不喜參與討論的學生，適時地提點並引導發言，對學生來說是利大於弊的。這類引導發言的英文用語頗為精簡，不需長篇大論便可發揮效用。比方說，簡單的一句 "Tell me more."、"What do you think?" 或 "You don't agree? Why not?" 等，就可引領同學講出更多意見喔！

在與學生互動溝通時，不論學生所提出的意見是好是壞，單單就有勇氣提出看法便值得嘉許。因此，針對學生意見的回覆應以正面鼓勵為佳，例如 "I like your ideas." 或 "I'm sure you can do it." 等，學生聽到皆可感受到教師的激勵。

作業的目的主要在讓學生有親自實作進而瞭解知識的機會，因此作業的設計與指派，除了科目知識之外，也可加入英語力學習的要素。舉例來說，請學生看一個 YouTube 上的英文影片，然後用英文口語表達看法；或是讓學生讀一篇英文的期刊文獻 (journal article) 之後，請他們用英文寫一篇簡短的摘要，如此便可有效地結合知識習得與英文練習兩者。

Notes

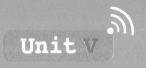

Interacting
with Students

教師與學生互動

⊤ Jessica. Have you started preparing for the exam?

潔西卡，妳開始準備考試了嗎？

ⓢ Yes. I've been reviewing my **notes**[1].

有的。我已經在複習一些筆記了。

ⓢ I'm interested in learning more about American history.

我有興趣瞭解更多關於美國的歷史。

⊤ You should check out the book *The Story of American Freedom* by Eric Foner.

那你應該看看埃里克‧方納所寫的《美國自由的故事》一書。

⊤ Instead of reading each individual word, you should try to develop a more effective reading strategy.

你應該想個有效的閱讀策略，而不是閱讀每個單字。

ⓢ I try to read for **gist**[2], but I'm not always sure I get the main idea of each passage.

我試著要讀文章大綱，但我並非很確定是否有讀懂文章的中心主旨。

⊙ TRACK **43**

S I know I need to study, but I just can't **concentrate**[3].
我知道我要認真，但就是無法集中注意力。

T You could start by **blocking**[4] **distracting**[5] apps and websites on your devices.
你不應該再看電子設備上那些會令人分心的程式和網站了。

T Okay, Michael. Why don't you share your ideas with us?
好的，麥可。請跟我們分享你的想法。

S Sure. I think businesses should not only provide high-quality products, but they should also offer excellent **customer**[6] service.
沒問題。我認為企業不僅應提供高品質的產品，還應該提供絕佳的客戶服務。

S So you want us to find reviews of the play we're reading, right?
所以您要我們找出目前所讀的劇本的評論，是嗎？

T **Exactly**[7], Melissa. I'm sure you could find some on the Internet, but I suggest visiting the school library. They have a lot of resources you won't find online.
沒錯，梅莉莎。我相信妳可以在網路上找到些資料，不過我也建議妳去學校圖書館找看看。那有一些資料是網路上沒有的呢。

T Don't listen passively. Try to be an **active**[8] listener.

不要只是被動地聽，要試著當主動有意識的聆聽者。

S Right. I've found some videos on YouTube explaining this skill.

是的，我已經在 YouTube 上找到一些解釋此技巧的影片。

S I think playing video games can help lower patients' **stress**[9] level.

我認為打電玩可讓病人減輕壓力。

T Okay, so what **evidence**[10] do you have supporting this idea?

好，那麼有什麼證據可支持此說法嗎？

T Anna, I've **noticed**[11] that you're now able to write quite complex sentences.

安娜，我發覺妳現在可以寫些較複雜的句子了。

S Yes, I've been practicing a lot.

是的，我有持續在大量練習。

S Whenever I present my ideas, I can never finish what I want to say within the time limit.

每次發表意見時，我總是無法在時間限制內把想說的都講完。

T Well, you should focus on the key points and then **time**[12] yourself while practicing.

嗯，那你應該挑要點講就好，並可在練習時幫自己計時呀。

Useful Tips

課堂之外與學生互動討論不僅能拉近師生的距離，教師也可針對學生的個別狀況給予學習意見。通常給意見回饋時，可參考以下幾個建議：

(1) 表示該建議是經由教師的實際觀察而提出，宜使用 "I've noticed that ..." 句型，避免 "They told me that ..." 等不明確的說法。
(2) 直截了當地提出建議，例如 "I suggest that you ..."，取代拐彎抹角的 "I didn't want to say this, but ..." 等說法。
(3) 可多使用正向鼓勵的話語，比方說 "You've been studying diligently. Great job." 等。

透過上述表達方式，學生可更明確瞭解應精進之技能，並在接受到鼓勵之後更有自信。

VOCABULARY

① notes (*n.*) 筆記
② gist (*n.*) 要旨；大意
③ concentrate (*v.*) 專心；集中
④ block (*v.*) 阻擋；封鎖
⑤ distracting (*adj.*) 使分散注意力的
⑥ customer (*n.*) 顧客

⑦ exactly (*adv.*) 確實；確切地
⑧ active (*adj.*) 積極的；主動的
⑨ stress (*n.*) 壓力
⑩ evidence (*n.*) 證據
⑪ notice (*v.*) 注意到
⑫ time (*v.*) 計時

T You did a wonderful job this **semester**[1], Linda.

琳達，這學期妳學得不錯喔。

S Thank you, Professor Wang. I did **devote**[2] a lot of time to the class.

謝謝您，王教授。我確實為這門課付出了很多時間。

S I got a B- on the assignment. How can I improve?

我的作業得了 B-。我該如何改進？

T Well, I suggest you include more **personal**[3] **views**[4] in your writing.

嗯，我建議你在文章中多加點個人的看法。

T Mary, you look a bit **lost**[5]. Are you sure you really understand this chapter?

瑪麗，妳看起來有點茫然。妳確定妳真的瞭解本章的概念嗎？

S Well, to be honest, I think the concept is a bit too **abstract**[6]. Could you provide some examples?

老實說，我覺得這概念有點太抽象。您能舉出一些例子嗎？

TRACK **45**

[S] I'm afraid I didn't do very well on the project.

恐怕我這個專題做得不是很好。

[T] It was a challenging task, and actually, I think you did some good work.

這個作業頗具挑戰性,其實我覺得你做得算還不錯耶。

[T] Kenny, you **scored**[7] pretty high on the math exam. Do you want to share your study strategies with the class?

肯尼,你數學考試分數考很高。你想與全班分享你的學習策略嗎?

[S] Sure, I'd love to.

當然。我很樂意。

[S] I'm thinking about taking five **courses**[8] next semester.

教授,我考慮下學期要選五門課。

[T] Five courses? Well, I'm afraid you're going to **struggle**[9] with the heavy **workload**[10].

五門課?我怕你會覺得課業過於繁重耶。

[T] Amanda, you clearly put in a lot of effort to complete all of the assignments. Great job.

亞曼達,妳很顯然是花了很多精神完成作業,很棒。

[S] Yes, but it was worth it. I really learned a lot.

是的,很值得呀!我還真的學到不少。

S Professor Murphy, how do you think my presentation went?

墨菲教授，您認為我的簡報如何？

T I thought it was great, Jerry. Very **professional**[11].

我認為很棒，傑瑞，很專業呀。

T I'm a bit **concerned about**[12] your reading skills. Do you want some help with that?

我對你的閱讀技巧感到有些擔心，你需要協助嗎？

S Thanks, but I'll try to read more on my own first.

謝謝，但我自己會先試著多閱讀的。

S I'd like to work on my writing skills.

我想增進寫作技巧。

T Okay, I've got an assignment for you. Select two articles from this book and write a 200-word summary for each.

好，那我給你個作業。從此書中選兩篇文章，各寫一篇兩百字的摘要。

Useful Tips

在評估學生的學習成效時，應盡量明確 (information-specific) 與聚焦 (issue-focused)。舉例說明，不要模糊地說 "You should read and write more."，而改以更明確地給出指令："Read three journal articles and write a one-page summary for each."。又比方說，不要將焦點發散如 "Everybody did a good job."，而應聚焦到明確的人與事："Linda, you used a variety of sentence structures in your essay. Great job."。如此，學生能更容易產生與教師的共鳴。

VOCABULARY

① semester (n.) 學期
② devote (v.) 奉獻
③ personal (adj.) 個人的
④ view (n.) 觀點；意見 (v.) 觀看
⑤ lost (adj.) 不知所措的；迷惘的
⑥ abstract (adj.) 抽象的
⑦ score (v.) 得分
⑧ course (n.) 課程
⑨ struggle (v.) 奮鬥；拼搏
⑩ workload (n.) 工作量
⑪ professional (adj.) 專業的
⑫ be concerned about 關心；擔心

S I couldn't sleep last night because I was thinking about this project. I'm just not sure how to start.

我昨晚一直想著專題的事都睡不著，我就是不知道要如何開始。

T You should start by doing some background reading.

你應該先從閱讀一些背景資料開始。

T Julie, have you had time to start planning your term project?

茱莉，妳有空開始計劃妳的學期專題了嗎？

S Yes, Professor Ito. I've decided to choose a topic **related**[1] to global warming.

有的，伊藤教授。我決定做全球暖化相關的議題。

S I'd better start preparing for the test, but I can't concentrate when studying **alone**[2].

我得趕快開始準備考試，但我一個人看書時無法集中注意力。

T Why don't you form a study group with a few other classmates?

你何不組一個學習小組和其他同學一起學習呢？

TRACK **47**

T Some companies have developed AI systems that can identify human emotions.

有些公司已經開發出可以辨識人類情緒的人工智慧系統了。

S Wow, that's interesting. How do they do that?

哇，真有趣。他們是怎麼做到的呀？

S I really need to improve my writing skills.

我真的需要精進我的寫作技巧。

T You should visit the writing center. The tutoring services they **offer**[3] are really helpful.

你可以去寫作中心查一下。他們提供的輔導服務相當有幫助。

T Simon, I think you've got a **talent**[4] for language learning.

賽門，我認為你在語言學習方面有很大的潛能。

S Thanks, Professor Chen. I've always wanted to be a **linguist**[5].

謝謝，陳教授。我一直想成為一名語言學家。

T Sarah, I'd love to see you be more **proactive**[6] in **spotting**[7] **grammar**[8] errors in your essays.

莎拉，我想請妳在寫論述文時多花些心力在文法正確性上。

S Okay, I'll **make an effort to**[9] **proofread**[10] my essays more carefully.

好的，我會多花點心思更仔細地校對。

S How can I improve my **memory**[11]? I mean, I understand the information but I **tend to**[12] forget it very quickly.

我要如何增進記憶力呀？我是說，資訊我都瞭解，但很快就忘記。

T Well, you can try to relate unfamiliar ideas to things you already know well.

你可以試著將不熟悉的資訊與已熟知的事物做連結。

S Whenever I need to give a presentation, I get tongue-tied and can't **express**[13] my ideas.

每當要做簡報，我表達意見時舌頭都會打結。

T Have you tried practicing in front of a mirror? Do that while **delivering**[14] your presentation a few times and you'll feel more **confident**[15].

你有沒有試過在鏡子前練習？在鏡子前把簡報內容練習多講幾次，你會感到比較有信心。

S Sometimes I **cram**[16] for an exam and get a pretty good score.

我有時在考試前會臨時抱佛腳，考試成績也滿不錯的。

T Well, cramming may work **in the short term**[17], but you probably won't remember much **afterwards**[18].

臨時抱佛腳對短期記憶有用，但之後會忘得很快。

VOCABULARY

① relate (*v.*) 有關；涉及
② alone (*adv.*) 單獨地；獨自地
③ offer (*v.*) 提供
④ talent (*n.*) 天分；天賦
⑤ linguist (*n.*) 語言學家
⑥ proactive (*adj.*) 積極的；主動的
⑦ spot (*v.*) 看出；發現
⑧ grammar (*n.*) 文法
⑨ make an effort to 努力～

⑩ proofread (*v.*) 校對
⑪ memory (*n.*) 記憶力
⑫ tend to 易於～
⑬ express (*v.*) 表達；陳述
⑭ deliver (*v.*) 發表
⑮ confident (*adj.*) 有信心的
⑯ cram (*v.*) 死記硬背
⑰ in the short term 短期地
⑱ afterwards (*adv.*) 此後；後來

S I'm looking for some ways to improve my English vocabulary.

我要想辦法增加英文單字量。

T Have you tried Boggle? It's an online vocabulary game that a lot of people use to expand their vocabulary.

你有沒有試過 Boggle？那是一款可擴充單字量的線上字彙遊戲，很多人都有用。

S Well, I don't have too much time to read.

我都沒太多時間閱讀。

T Why don't you download audiobooks on your smartphone so you can listen anywhere?

你何不試試下載有聲書到手機上呢？這樣就隨處可聽了。

S I have a hard time organizing my notes.

我很不會整理筆記。

T You can use the Clear-Notes app to organize your classroom notes into virtual notepads.

你可以使用 Clear-Notes 這個 app 來將課堂筆記整理到雲端的記事本上。

⊙ TRACK **49**

S When I study alone, I just can't concentrate.

我一個人看書就無法專心。

T I suggest that you join a study group. You can review materials and exchange ideas with other students.

我建議你參加讀書會。你可以跟其他同學一起複習資料和交換意見。

S I prefer to use print dictionaries.

我比較喜歡使用紙本字典。

T I know, me too. Print dictionaries don't have ads so you won't get distracted.

我瞭解,我也是。紙本字典沒有廣告,不會因此分心。

S Can you **recommend**[1] a good book for me to read?

您可以推薦必讀好書嗎?

T You're interested in geography, right? Then I recommend *Hello! Geography*. It's a real **page-turner**[2].

你對地理有興趣,對吧?那我推薦你看《Hello! Geography》這本。你會愛不釋手。

S How can I improve my English listening skills?

我要如何增進英聽能力呢?

T I strongly suggest you listen to English podcasts. There's a good one called *All in English*.

我強烈建議你聽英文播客。有個叫作「All in English」的播客不錯喔!

S Do you recommend any online **encyclopedias**[3]?

您可推薦線上百科全書嗎？

T Yes. *Encyclopedia Britannica* is **certainly**[4] a good one.

可以呀，「Encyclopedia Britannica」的確是個不錯的選擇。

S I'm trying to get a higher TOEFL score.

我的托福想考高分一點。

T Then you have to familiarize yourself with a few important test taking strategies.

那你就要對重要的考試技巧很熟練。

S I need some **tips**[5] for improving my spoken English.

我需要一些幫助改善英文口說能力的訣竅。

T Try to speak as much as possible and express your opinions freely without worrying about sentence **structure**[6] or grammar.

試著盡量多講，先不要擔心句型和文法，自由地發表意見就好。

Useful Tips

教師給予學習建議時應盡量明確具體。除了傳統教材外，若能整合線上工具提供實用的應用程式 (app)、網站 (website)，甚至相關影音 (audio/video、authentic materials/resources) 等資料給學生參考則更佳。

VOCABULARY

① recommend (*v.*) 推薦
② page-turner (*n.*) 引人入勝的書
③ encyclopedia (*n.*) 百科全書
④ certainly (*adv.*) 確實；無疑地
⑤ tip (*n.*) 指點；指導
⑥ structure (*n.*) 結構

討論職涯方向

Career Exploration

T → **Teacher**   S → **Student**

T What do you plan to do after **graduation**[1]?
你畢業後打算做什麼？

S Well, I just feel like I need a bit of a **rest**[2]. I might **go backpacking**[3] around Southeast Asia.
嗯，我覺得我需要休息一下。我可能會去東南亞國家背包旅行。

S I don't really want to **get stuck in**[4] a 9-to-5 job.
我真的不想困在朝九晚五的工作中耶。

T I think you've got some academic potential. You may want to think about **enrolling**[5] in a master's program.
我覺得你很有學術上的潛力，你可以考慮申請研究所呀。

T Are you ready to go out and find a job, Joe?
你準備好要找工作了嗎，喬？

S Well, finding a job is hard for me, since I don't have much on my **resume**[6] yet.
嗯，找工作對我來說有點困難，因為我的簡歷還不是很豐富。

[S] I heard that a job **fair**[7] will be held at the school next week, right?

我聽說下週學校要舉辦就業博覽會，是嗎？

[T] Oh, yeah. A **recruitment**[8] fair organized by the Career Center. You definitely should go and learn more about job and **internship**[9] **opportunities**[10].

噢，對啊。是就業中心安排的招募會。你一定要去瞭解更多關於工作和實習機會的資訊。

[T] Helen, you can find free online courses through the Coursera platform.

海倫，妳可以透過 Coursera 平台找到免費的線上課程。

[S] Thank you so much. I've always wanted to learn more about nursing.

非常感謝。我一直想多學點護理知識。

[S] I'm still **confused**[11] about my **career path**[12].

我對自己的職涯規劃仍感到有些迷惘。

[T] You can talk to the school's career **counselors**[13]. They can help you **figure out**[14] what your **strengths**[15] are.

你可以和學校內的職涯顧問談談。他們可以協助你找出你的優勢。

[T] Don't worry. You've still got time to decide what to do after graduating.

別擔心。你還有時間可以決定畢業後要做什麼。

[S] Yeah, for now I'm just planning to attend some **networking**[16] **events**[17] and meet some people in the **industry**[18].

是的，現階段我打算參加一些社交活動認識業界的朋友。

S I need someone to **spruce up**[19] my CV and help me **brush up**[20] my **interview**[21] skills.

我需要有人協助我美化履歷表並加強面試技巧。

T I'm happy to help, Henry.

我很樂意幫助你，亨利。

T Carol. You mentioned that you want to become an **influencer**[22]?

卡蘿。妳提到說妳想當網紅？

S Yes, I do. I've created what I think is a pretty good LinkedIn **profile**[23] and started my own YouTube **channel**[24].

對呀。我剛建立了我自覺還不錯的 LinkedIn 個人資料並開設了自己的 YouTube 頻道。

S I want to identify my working style. Do you know where I can take a **personality**[25] test?

我想確認自己的工作風格。您知道我在哪裡可以做性格測試嗎？

T Yes. You can **contact**[26] Ms. Sherry Lee at the Career Resource Center.

嗯，你可以跟職涯資源中心的李雪莉小姐聯絡。

VOCABULARY

① graduation (n.) 畢業
② rest (n.) 休息（時間）；休養
③ go backpacking 背包旅行
④ get stuck in 陷入～
⑤ enroll (v.) 登記；參加
⑥ resume (n.) 履歷表
⑦ fair (n.) 展覽會
⑧ recruitment (n.) 招聘
⑨ internship (n.) 實習
⑩ opportunity (n.) 機會
⑪ confused (adj.) 困惑的
⑫ career path 職涯規劃
⑬ counselor (n.) 顧問

⑭ figure out 找出
⑮ strength (n.) 優點；強項
⑯ networking (n.) 人脈網絡建立
⑰ event (n.) 活動
⑱ industry (n.) 產業
⑲ spruce up 打點整齊
⑳ brush up 複習
㉑ interview (n.) 採訪；面試；會見
㉒ influencer (n.) 網紅
㉓ profile (n.) 人物簡介
㉔ channel (n.) 頻道
㉕ personality (n.) 性格
㉖ contact (v.) 聯絡

Unit VI

Peer Interactions

學生之間的交流

M → Male   F → Female

M Hey, Angie. How have you been?

嘿，安潔。近來可好？

F Not too bad. How about you, Ethan?

不錯呀。你呢，伊森？

F Charles, I didn't see you at the **dorm**[1] yesterday.

查爾斯，我昨天在宿舍沒看到你耶。

M Oh, I was at the library all day collecting information for my presentation.

噢，我整天都在圖書館收集資料準備簡報。

M Laura, do you live on or off **campus**[2]?

蘿拉，妳住校內還是校外呀？

F I share a house near school with three other students.

我在學校附近跟另外三個同學分租一間房子。

TRACK **53**

F Oh, hi, Andy. You're taking Academic Writing, too?

噢，嗨，安迪。你也修學術寫作課喔？

M Yes, it's my only elective this semester.

對呀，這是我這學期唯一的選修課。

M Hey, Maggie. Have you got time to discuss the term project?

嘿，瑪姬。妳有空可討論學期專題嗎？

F Yeah, sure. My next class isn't until 4:30 so I've got about an hour. That should be enough time.

可以呀。我下一堂課是四點半，所以還有大約一小時，應該夠吧。

F I really like the **lounge**³ in the student center.

我很喜歡學生中心的休息室耶。

M Me too. It's one of my favorite places to **hang out**⁴ between classes.

我也喜歡。那是我課堂中間打發時間最喜歡去的地方之一。

F Justin, can I ask you about the research report over lunch?

賈斯汀，我能利用午餐時間問你關於研究報告的事嗎？

M Sure. Why don't we meet at the student **cafeteria**⁵ at 12:30?

當然。我們何不十二點半在學生餐廳碰面？

M Natalie, why are you in such a hurry?

娜塔莉，妳為什麼這麼趕？

F Oh, hi, Hans. I'm almost late for class. I'll talk to you later, okay?

噢，嗨，漢斯。我上課快要遲到了。晚點聊，OK？

M Hello, Michelle. Can I join you guys?

哈囉，蜜雪兒。我可以加入你們嗎？

F Sure, Bill. Have a seat. So, what's for lunch? Oh, you're having a sandwich.

當然，比爾。坐吧。你午餐吃什麼？噢，你吃三明治喔。

F Josh, hey, wait up a minute. You walk so fast.

喬許，嘿，等等我呀。你走得真快。

M Oh, hi, Patty. Yeah, sorry. I'm running late, and Jackson Hall is pretty far from here.

噢，嗨，佩蒂。不好意思，我快遲到了。傑克森館離這還真遠。

VOCABULARY

① dorm (*n.*) 宿舍 (= dormitory)
② campus (*n.*) 校園
③ lounge (*n.*) 休息室
④ hang out 消磨時間；出去玩
⑤ cafeteria (*n.*) 自助餐廳

TRACK **55**

M → **Male**   F → **Female**

M Lily, are you going to the student **association**[1] party this weekend?

莉莉，妳要參加學生會在本週末舉辦的派對嗎？

F I'm afraid I can't. I'm going to be all tied up with school projects.

恐怕沒辦法。我做學校專題忙翻了。

F Classes start next week, but I just can't find the chemistry textbook. All the bookstores say it's **out of stock**[2].

下週就要開始上課了，但我就是找不到化學課本。所有書店都說那本書缺貨了。

M Don't worry. You can download the ebook from the library.

別擔心。妳可以從圖書館下載電子書呀。

M There are only five students in my pragmatics class.

語用學那班只有五個學生耶。

F That's good. You'll get a lot of individual attention from the professor.

那很好呀。你會得到教授個別的關注。

VOCABULARY

① association (*n.*) 協會
② out of stock 缺貨；沒庫存

F Do you want to get something to eat at the coffee shop?

你想不想去咖啡館吃些東西？

M Well, I don't really like their cakes and muffins. They're a bit dry and don't really have any **flavor**[3].

嗯，我不是很喜歡那裡的蛋糕和瑪芬。我覺得有點乾，而且也沒有什麼味道。

M Sandra, I'm thinking about **transferring**[4], but I'm still not too sure.

珊卓，我在考慮轉學耶，不過還不是很確定啦。

F What? Why would you want to leave York University? I thought you liked it here.

什麼？你怎麼會想離開約克大學呢？我以為你喜歡這裡耶。

F You look **awful**[5], Bobby. Are you okay?

你看起來很糟耶，巴比。你還好嗎？

M Well, some students in the dorm were playing music all night. I didn't get much sleep.

嗯，宿舍裡的一些學生整晚都在放音樂。吵得我睡也睡不好呀。

M **Orientation**[6] for first-year students will be held next Friday.

一年級學生的迎新活動將於下週五舉行。

F It sounds like a good chance for new students to get to know each other.

看來這是新生認識彼此的絕佳機會。

VOCABULARY

③ flavor (*n.*) 味道

④ transfer (*v.*) 轉校；轉系

⑤ awful (*adj.*) 極壞的；糟糕的

⑥ orientation (*n.*) 培訓

F The deadline for **declaring**[7] a major is next week, but I still don't know what I want to major in.

選擇主修科目的截止日期就是下週了，但我還不清楚要主修什麼耶。

M Well, neither do I. I guess it's common for **freshmen**[8] like us.

嗯，我也還沒決定。我們新生會有這種感覺也算是正常。

M The cafeteria is serving special meals prepared by the school's **culinary**[9] arts students today.

今天學校餐廳會供應我們學校烹飪系學生所準備的特別餐點耶。

F Let's check it out. I don't know if it's going to be good, but I'm sure it's good practice for the students in the program.

那我們去看看呀。餐點好不好吃我是不知道啦，但我想這對於那系上的學生來說是個很棒的練習機會。

F Adam, would you be interested in **working part-time**[10] off campus?

亞當，你對在校外打工有興趣嗎？

M I'd love to. I could really use the money.

我很想呀。我還真需要賺點錢。

VOCABULARY

⑦ declare (*v.*) 表明
⑧ freshman (*n.*) 大學一年級生；新生
⑨ culinary (*adj.*) 烹飪的
⑩ work part-time 做兼職工作

M → Male   F → Female

M Wow, brand new textbooks are really expensive. I'm definitely going to stick to used books instead.

哇，全新的課本好貴喔。我打定主意要買二手書就好。

F Yes, they're cheaper of course, but they sell out quickly.

是呀，當然是會便宜些，但很快就賣光了。

M I don't know what courses I should take. Ann, can you help me with this?

我不知道我應該修什麼課耶。安，妳能幫我看看嗎？

F Not really. You should meet with your academic **advisor**[1], Tobey.

不好吧，你應該去問你的指導老師呀，陶比。

M The professor mentioned the final project will be an oral presentation, right?

教授有提到期末專題是要做口頭簡報，對嗎？

F Yes, we're supposed to **select**[2] a topic and start researching it this week.

是的，我們應該要先選個主題，這禮拜內就開始找資料。

VOCABULARY

① advisor (*n.*) 顧問；指導者
② select (*v.*) 選擇

🔘 TRACK **57**

M I'm not sure I understand the **grading system**[3]. Do you?

我對給分標準不是很瞭解，妳呢？

F I think it's pretty **straightforward**[4]. The **midterm**[5] and final exams account for 60% of the final grade and the presentation accounts for 40%.

我看很簡單呀。期中和期末考試佔總成績的六成，簡報佔四成。

M My chemistry class is being taught by a teaching assistant, but I'd rather it be taught by an **experienced**[6] professor.

我的化學課是由助教上課耶，但我希望是有經驗的教授來教。

F Come on. A lot of the teaching assistants here are more **enthusiastic**[7] than the professors.

拜託。這邊很多助教比教授更有教學熱忱耶。

M The first opinion essay is **due**[8] on Friday, isn't it? I don't think I can get it done by then.

第一份意見論文要在週五交，對嗎？我覺得我可能寫不完耶。

F Maybe you can talk to the professor and ask for an extension.

也許你可以和教授談談，看能不能延後交。

VOCABULARY

③ grading system 評分制度
④ straightforward (*adj.*) 易懂的
⑤ midterm (*n.*) 期中考試

⑥ experienced (*adj.*) 有經驗的
⑦ enthusiastic (*adj.*) 熱心的
⑧ due (*adj.*) 應給的

M I always bring my **laptop**[9] to class. Taking notes on the computer is just quicker and easier.

我都會帶筆記型電腦去上課。在電腦上做筆記就是更快更方便。

F Yeah, and I use mine to **look up**[10] background information on whatever the professor is talking about.

對呀，不管教授講什麼主題，我都用電腦查找相關的背景資料。

M Are we really supposed to finish viewing all three of the assigned videos before the class?

我們真的要在上課前看完教授指定的三段影片？

F Yeah, the professor said that if you don't know what the videos are about, you won't be able to contribute to the class discussion.

沒錯，教授說如果不先瞭解那些影片內容的話，上課時就沒辦法參與討論了。

M Let's work on these vocabulary questions together.

我們一起做這些詞彙問題吧。

F Sure. We need to **match**[11] the words on the left with the correct meanings on the right.

好呀，我們要將左邊的字詞和右邊的正確意思配對起來。

. VOCABULARY
⑨ laptop (*n.*) 筆記型電腦
⑩ look up 查詢
⑪ match (*v.*) 配對

Ⓜ Nicole, do you have time to discuss the project now?

妮可，妳現在有空可以討論一下專題嗎？

Ⓕ Let's do it. It says here that we have to **investigate**[12] the **correlation**[13] between children's brain development and their language **proficiency**[14].

我們來討論吧。這邊說我們要研究兒童大腦發育和他們的語言能力之間的關係。

VOCABULARY

⑫ investigate (*v.*) 調查
⑬ correlation (*n.*) 相關性
⑭ proficiency (*n.*) 精通；熟練

M → Male   F → Female

M The student exchange program is accepting applications for next year. Are you going to apply?

明年的交換學生計劃已經開始申請了耶，妳要去申請嗎？

F Yeah, we're not going to have a better chance to get out and explore a different **culture**[1].

要呀，沒有比這更能出國探索不同文化的大好機會了。

F Can you help me? I need to find a place to live for the **upcoming**[2] semester.

你能幫幫我嗎？我要找個下學期可住的地方。

M It's a bit late now. We don't have any rooms available in the student dorms.

現在已經有點晚了耶。學生宿舍都沒有空房了。

M Well, I just heard that evening classes won't be available starting next semester.

我剛聽說從下學期開始就沒有夜間課程可選了耶。

F Oh, no. I have a 9-to-5 job and can only take evening classes.

噢，不會吧。我有個朝九晚五的工作，我也只能上夜間的課呀。

VOCABULARY

① culture (*n.*) 文化

② upcoming (*adj.*) 即將來臨的

TRACK **59**

F I'm going to put up some posters promoting my reading group outside the student center.

我要在學生中心外張貼一些海報來宣傳我的閱讀社團。

M You didn't know? Students are no longer allowed to post anything on the wall there.

妳不知道嗎？學校已不再允許學生在那裡的牆上張貼任何東西了耶。

M Are student plays open to the general public?

我們的學生戲劇表演有開放給一般社會大眾觀賞嗎？

F Yes, and the tickets are free. That's how we get such large audiences.

有呀，免費索票。這就是我們招攬到那麼多觀眾的方式。

F There will be new personal study **cubicles**[3] **installed**[4] in the library next week.

下週圖書館將會安裝新的個人讀書隔間耶。

M That's wonderful. It's impossible for me to focus when I'm sitting at those big open tables.

那太棒了。我坐在開放空間的大桌上看書就是無法專心呀。

VOCABULARY

③ cubicle (*n.*) 小隔間　　　　　　④ install (*v.*) 安裝

M Good news, Camila. Starting spring semester, free **tutoring**[5] will be available to all students.

好消息，卡蜜拉。從春季學期開始，所有學生都有免費輔導服務耶。

F Really? Wow, that's wonderful. I really need this. I mean ... I need extra help with biology.

真的嗎？哇，太棒了。我真的很需要。我是說……我需要有人來救救我的生物課。

F I was told that the university has decided to **discontinue**[6] the free bus service.

有人跟我說學校決定要停止免費巴士服務了。

M I know. I **guess**[7] it's because the buses are too expensive to **operate**[8].

我知道呀。我猜是因為巴士運營成本太高了吧。

M I can't believe it. I was **charged**[9] an extra $100 for using the gym on campus this morning.

我簡直不敢相信。今天早上我去校內健身房被多收了一百塊使用費。

F They say it's because the school needs money to **upgrade**[10] the **workout**[11] **equipment**[12].

他們說這是因為學校需要資金來升級健身器材。

VOCABULARY

⑤ tutor (*v.*) 輔導；指導
⑥ discontinue (*v.*) 停止；終止
⑦ guess (*v.*) 猜想
⑧ operate (*v.*) 營運

⑨ charge (*v.*) 收費
⑩ upgrade (*v.*)（使）升級
⑪ workout (*n.*) 健身
⑫ equipment (*n.*) 設備

M The school cafeteria is going to start **broadcasting**[13] English news programs during mealtimes now.

校內的學生餐廳開始在用餐時間播放英語新聞節目了耶。

F Well, that's not a bad idea. At least not for those of us who want to **immerse**[14] ourselves in an English environment.

嗯，這個主意還不錯呀。至少對我們這些想沉浸在英語環境中的人是好消息。

VOCABULARY

⑬ broadcast (v.) 播放；廣播
⑭ immerse (v.) 使浸沒；使埋首於

M → **Male**   F → **Female**

F Today's Academic Writing class will be conducted **via**[1] Webex, right?

今天的學術寫作課將透過 Webex 進行，對嗎？

M Yeah. The professor sent out an email with the invite, so you can just click on the link.

沒錯。教授已透過電郵發送邀請了，所以妳只要點連結就好。

F How can I submit my opinion essay? Should I print it out or ...?

我要怎麼交意見論文呀？要印出來還是……？

M No. You should upload the file to the class's shared folder.

不用。把檔案上傳到班級共享資料夾內就好。

F Hey, Brian. The meeting **code**[2] for our online history class is "UND-WZH", right? How come I can't sign in?

嘿，布萊恩。我們線上歷史課的會議代碼是 "UND-WZH"，對嗎？我怎麼都無法登入呢？

M Doris, the new code is "AOR-XUQ". The professor changed it ten minutes ago.

桃樂絲，新代碼是 "AOR-XUQ"。教授十分鐘前才改的。

VOCABULARY

① via (*prep.*) 經由；透過
② code (*n.*) 代碼

🔘 TRACK **61**

F It's my turn to present the chapter summary during our online **session**[3] today. Can you show me how I can share my screen?

今天的網課，輪到我報告章節要點了。你能教我怎麼分享螢幕嗎？

M Of course. You see this "screen" icon on top? Click on it and everyone will be able to see your slides.

好呀。妳看到上方的這個「螢幕」圖標了嗎？點一下，每個人就都可以看到妳的投影片了。

F I heard that the online **seminars**[4] this semester will all be three hours long.

聽說這個學期的線上研討課都是三個小時耶。

M Really? Most students cannot concentrate for three hours **straight**[5].

真的嗎？多數學生的注意力沒辦法持續三個小時吧。

VOCABULARY

③ session (*n.*) 學期；上課期間；講習
④ seminar (*n.*) 研討班；專題討論會
⑤ straight (*adv.*) 連續地；不間斷地

M I really **prefer**[6] to attend classes online. Just think how much **commuting**[7] time I've saved.

我真的滿喜歡上網課耶。光節省下的通勤時間就不知多少了。

F **Indeed**[8]. And I've found that I actually concentrate better when taking online courses.

的確是。我也覺得上網課時反而還更專心耶。

F Okay, Phil. We're both in group A. So, we should analyze the first business case study, right?

好，菲爾。我們倆都是 A 組。那我們應該分析第一個商業案例，對吧？

M Yes, I think so. Let's have a look at the Padlet and see what the case is about.

我想是吧。我們上去 Padlet 看看那案例是關於什麼。

M Lisa, what did you think of the online **workshop**[9] yesterday?

麗莎，妳覺得昨天那場線上工作坊怎麼樣？

F I thought it was really **helpful**[10]. It's already changed how I'm planning to analyze the data I've collected.

我覺得對我幫助極大。那讓我對如何計劃分析所收集到的資料有不同的認識。

F The history class this afternoon will be conducted on Webex.

今天下午的歷史課會在 Webex 上進行喔。

M Ugh. I thought the professor preferred MS Teams. Oh well, I guess I'll have to install the Webex application before class.

呃。我以為教授比較喜歡用 MS Teams 咧。好吧，我想我還是得必須在上課前先把 Webex 應用程式安裝好。

M I know we're expected to complete evaluations of our professors, but how?

我知道我們要寫對教授們的評鑑，但如何完成呀？

F You can **log in**[11] to the school system and do it online.

你要登入學校系統，在線上就可以寫了。

VOCABULARY

⑥ prefer (*v.*) 較喜歡
⑦ commute (*v.*) 通勤
⑧ indeed (*adv.*) 的確；實在
⑨ workshop (*n.*) 工作坊
⑩ helpful (*adj.*) 有助益的
⑪ log in 登入

Notes

Talking About Online Learning

論線上教學 表達觀點特訓

後疫情時代,雖說線上授課儼然已成為常態且許多師生也有「回不去了」的感覺,但如同所有事物一樣,線上課程也有優缺點與正反兩面評價。很多時候有機會與其他教師或跟同學討論到自己對線上課程的看法,此時若心中有點子便可侃侃而談。本單元的目的便是歸納要點,幫助讀者暢言無礙!

我是教師
For
Teachers

線上教學的優點
Advantages of Online Learning

首先是以口語表達線上教學的優點，或是即便遇到困難阻礙，也可派上用場的解決方案等。

☐ When students view my pre-recorded lectures, they can learn at their own pace and review lessons as many times as necessary.

當學生們觀看我預先錄製的課程時，他們可以按照自己的步調學習，並根據個人需求複習課程。

☐ I've set up online **peer**[1] groups where students can exchange ideas and get **support**[2] from each other.

我建立了線上學習小組，學生們可以在小組內交換意見並互相支援與討論。

☐ I usually have my Google Meet sessions recorded so that students can view or listen to lessons again and again.

我通常使用 Google Meet 上課時會錄影，以便讓學生們可以無數次地觀看或收聽課程。

☐ I especially enjoy engaging students by **integrating**[3] all sorts of online teaching tools, like Padlet, Kahoot!, and Slido, into my classes.

我特別喜歡在課堂中整合各種線上教學工具，例如：Padlet、Kahoot! 和 Slido，來吸引學生。

☐ Since online classes can be conducted from home, I really save on travel time, which I sometimes use to plan extra activities.

由於線上課程可以在家進行，我的確節省了不少通勤時間並可利用時間規劃更多課程活動。

☐ Whenever I need to **update**[4] my teaching materials, I simply log in to the online teaching platform and upload the corrected version.

每當我需要更新教材時,我只須登入線上教學平台就可將修正過的版本上傳。

Sentence Pattern

Whenever I need to ..., I ... 每當我需要……,我便……

⑩ Whenever I need to communicate with students, I use i-Send to send messages.

每當我要與學生互動,我就使用 i-Send 來傳送訊息。

Useful Tips

線上課程的優點就是不受時地等限制,隨時開個 Google Meet 或 Webex 會議室便可進入虛擬教室上課、互動,師生彼此所節省下的來回交通時間,還可做更妥善的運用,例如教師規劃課程或批改學生作業等。因此,若論及線上課程的優點,可朝更有彈性方面(人員、地點、時間等)發想。

VOCABULARY

① peer (*n.*) 同儕
② support (*n./v.*) 支持
③ integrate (*v.*) 使合併;使成為一體;整合
④ update (*v.*) 更新

線上教學的缺點
Disadvantages of Online Learning

線上教學有其彈性的優點，也有可能造成不便的缺點。例如網路不穩或缺乏師生互動等，下列說法都有助於針對線上教學不足之處抒發感想。

☐ My online classes **occasionally**[1] start late because of some technical issues.

因為技術上的問題，我的線上課程有時會延後開始。

☐ I don't really have much experience with this online course technology.

我對這種線上課程的工具不是很熟練。

☐ Well, screen sharing is always **laggy**[2] and I find it's pretty **ineffective**[3].

嗯，螢幕分享總是會卡卡的，我覺得使用起來效果不佳。

☐ It's rather difficult to keep students **engaged**[4] in online classes. They get **distracted**[5] very easily.

要在線上課程中讓學生參與難度大增，他們很容易就分心。

☐ Well, the **unstable**[6] Internet connection really drives us crazy. Every so often students suddenly just get **disconnected**[7].

網路不穩定的話真的會讓我們抓狂。三不五時總會有學生突然斷線。

☐ I'm having some technical difficulties now, so it might be a few minutes until we get started. Sorry about that.

我現在遇到了點技術問題，所以我們稍晚開始。非常不好意思。

⊡ TRACK **64**

Sentence Pattern

● **I don't really have much experience with [something].**
我並沒有很多使用〔某物〕的經驗。

⊚ I don't really have much experience with this Webex application.
我對此 Webex 應用程式的使用不甚熟悉。

Useful Tips

不可諱言，線上課程縱使有彈性，但有些教師或學生還是認為使用工具
軟體有其限制或不便，但與其抱怨問題，不如積極地尋找解決方案。
比方說有些教師認為網課互動性不高，建議多多善用互動工具，例如
Slido 或 Kahoot! 等，來與學生問答以增加互動性。

VOCABULARY

① occasionally (*adv.*) 有時候
② laggy (*adj.*) 延遲的；〔電腦〕
反應慢的
③ ineffective (*adj.*) 無效率的

④ engaged (*adj.*) 參與的；忙於某事的
⑤ distracted (*adj.*) 分心的
⑥ unstable (*adj.*) 不穩的
⑦ disconnect (*v.*) 切斷（電源、線路等）

討論線上教學的優缺點──教師視角

A: Hey, Professor Lin. How's everything?

B: Not too bad. Well, actually I'm pretty busy with the online course planning. I mean ... I'm still not too **familiar**[1] with those platforms, you know ... like, Webex, Zoom, and all the other tools.

A: Yeah, I know what you're saying. Learning how to use all those online tools can be challenging, right?

B: Indeed. I really have no idea how to start. Do I have to learn them all, or what?

A: Well, I suggest that you start with Google Meet since it's quite easy to use and the interface is pretty straightforward.

B: Does it have screen sharing?

A: Yes, of course. Just about every online teaching platform has that **feature**[2]. You can even choose to present your entire screen or just a window.

B: Oh, that's wonderful. Thank you for sharing.

A: Sure, no problem. Well, I can show you how it works, if you want me to.

B: That's okay. I think I'll try to figure it out myself. Thanks again.

○ **VOCABULARY**
① familiar (*adj.*) 熟悉的
② feature (*n.*) 特徵；特色

A：嗨，林教授。最近還好嗎？

B：還可以。嗯，事實上，線上課程規劃一事讓我忙翻了。我是說……我對這些線上課程平台都不甚熟悉呀，妳知道的，像是 Webex、Zoom 和一些其他工具。

A：是的，我瞭解。學習如何使用這些線上工具還有點挑戰性，對吧？

B：的確。我真不知道我應該從何著手。我要全都學會還是怎的？

A：嗯，我建議你可以從 Google Meet 著手，因為它非常易於使用且界面頗為簡單。

B：有分享螢幕的功能嗎？

A：當然有呀。幾乎所有的線上課程平台都有這功能呀。你甚至還可以選擇顯示整個螢幕或是僅顯示一個視窗。

B：噢，那太好了。謝謝妳的分享。

A：不客氣。如果你要我操作給你看也可以的。

B：沒關係。我想我可以試著自己弄清楚。再次謝謝妳喔。

⊙ TRACK **66**

A: Hello, Professor Cheng. How are your online courses going?

B: Oh, hey, Professor Cole. I love conducting courses online!

A: Great. What do you like about it?

B: Just think how much commuting time I've **saved**[1]. Well, I mean ... I can sit at home and start my classes with just a few clicks.

A: Yeah, it's certainly very convenient.

B: Also, I can record the whole class session for those students who are unable to attend.

A: Exactly. A simple click on the "Record" icon and the entire class can be **documented**[2].

B: But don't you feel that you and your students are **separated**[3] by a screen?

A: Well, I ask all my students to turn on their webcams to try to create that "in-person" feeling, you know?

B: Yeah, I understand. No matter what we think about them, virtual classes have become the new **normal**[4] for teachers and students.

VOCABULARY

① save (*v.*) 節省；儲存
② document (*v.*) 記錄
③ separate (*v.*) 分隔；分開
④ normal (*n.*) 標準；常態

A：妳好，程教授。妳的線上課程進展如何？

B：噢，嗨，科爾教授。我真的超愛線上授課耶！

A：不錯喔。妳喜歡什麼部分呢？

B：光想我節省的通勤時間就不知多少了。嗯，我的意思是……我可以坐在家裡，在電腦上點幾個功能鍵就可以開始上課了。

A：對啊，的確很方便。

B：而且，我還可以把整堂課錄下來給缺席的學生看。

A：沒錯。只須點一下「錄影」鍵，就可以錄製整個課程了。

B：但是你不覺得你和學生被螢幕分隔了嗎？

A：嗯，我要求所有的學生都將鏡頭打開，並試著創造出一種「面對面」的感覺，妳懂吧？

B：是啊，我懂。不過，無論我們感覺如何，虛擬課程已成為教師和學生的學習新常態了。

線上教學的優點

Advantages of Online Learning

在台灣，為達成 2030 年雙語國家的發展目標，不僅學生還有教師也應精益求精，不斷提升自己的英文程度和授課能力，因此通過英檢 B2[註]等級也是必不可少的。目前較適合教師增能的英檢以 GEPT 高級、IELTS 與 TOEFL 為主要項目，而此三者皆有測驗寫作能力。因此，本單元分享的是給教師們參考的描述網路課程之優點的文章寫法。

Example

I believe that the move to online classes has **drastically**[1] changed the way teachers teach and **manage**[2] classes.

To begin with, conducting classes online tends to be more effective than teaching in the **traditional**[3] way. For example, before the online sessions begin, I usually have all of the reading materials uploaded to the system and **distributed**[4] to students ahead of time. This way, students have **sufficient**[5] time to preview the lessons and are better prepared to contribute ideas during online sessions. Some of my students mention that it's easy to access journal articles from a shared folder and they can view those required reading materials on any device at any time. With the help of technology, teachers can **engage**[6] students more actively.

Second, setting "rules" for online classes is **relatively**[7] easy for teachers. For example, I can require my students to stay on mute when not talking, ask questions in the chat box, or click on the "Raise Hand" icon to indicate they want to voice their opinion. In addition, being able to automatically assign students to different discussion groups is simply my favorite feature of online teaching. Not only can I allocate time for peer or group discussions, but I can also join different groups to ensure that the students are keeping the discussion on track. All in all, virtual-classroom management can be done more **effortlessly**[8] than traditional classroom management.

我相信線上課程已徹底改變了教師教學和管理課堂的方式。

首先，線上授課往往比傳統方式教學更有效。例如，線上課程開始之前，我通常會將所有文獻上傳到學校系統並提前發送給學生。如此，學生就有足夠的時間來預讀教材，從而在事先準備之後便可在線上課程中提出想法。我的一些學生也提到從共享資料夾存取文章很簡便，他們可以隨時在任何設備上查看指定的閱讀素材。在科技的協助之下，教師可以更積極地吸引學生參與。

再者，對於教師來說，為線上課程制定「規則」相對容易得多。例如，我可以要求學生在不發言時保持靜音，在聊天框中提出問題，或點擊「舉手」圖標以表明他們想表達意見。此外，將學生分配到不同討論小組的功能簡直是我的最愛。我不僅可以為兩人討論或小組討論分配時間，而且我還能加入不同的小組，以確保學生的討論都沒有離題。總而言之，與傳統課堂管理相比，虛擬課堂管理能夠更輕鬆地完成。

註：B2 等級是依據語言能力評量標準 CEFR（Common European Framework of Reference for Languages 歐洲語言共同參考架構）。各類英檢成績參考對應表見 P.173。

⊙ TRACK **67**

● **Not only V. + S., but S. + (also) + V.** 不僅……，還……

⑩ Not only is Mr. King **articulate**[9], but he also has personal **charisma**[10].

金恩先生不僅能言善道，他還擁有個人魅力。

Grammar

Not only 置於句首時，其後的主詞與動詞位置會對調，形成「倒裝」句型。但請注意，but ... 後的子句則不用倒裝！

⑩ Not only should we recruit more service representatives, but we should also consider expanding internationally.

我們不僅要招聘更多的服務代表，還要考慮拓展業務到海外去。

⑩ Not only can Vera sing beautifully, but she can also dance elegantly.

薇拉不僅歌聲優美，而且跳舞也很優雅。

Useful Tips

以教師較進階的英文程度，寫作上可運用一些特殊句型，像是上述提及的「倒裝句」等。當然，這是指自身在練習或準備 B2 英檢考試時可運用，若是指導學生時，還是要依照其程度使用簡單明確的句型，未必要要求每位學生都使用進階的倒裝句。

○ VOCABULARY

① drastically (*adv.*) 劇烈地
② manage (*v.*) 管理
③ traditional (*adj.*) 傳統的
④ distribute (*v.*) 散佈；廣發
⑤ sufficient (*adj.*) 充分的

⑥ relatively (*adv.*) 相較地
⑦ engage (*v.*) 吸引；使參與
⑧ effortlessly (*adv.*) 不費力地
⑨ articulate (*adj.*) 善於表達的
⑩ charisma (*n.*) 個人魅力；吸引力

線上教學的缺點
Disadvantages of Online Learning

英文寫作力求層次分明，且內容言之有物，論述讓人一看就懂，這可比使用美侖美奐的莎翁級單字來的實際多了；架構方面，除了在首句點出自己的立場之外，主要論述段落也分別應有主題句 (topic sentence) 和舉例 (examples)，此即所有主流英檢測驗所要求的明確架構。

Example

Of course, some teachers are feeling pretty proud that they've been able to conduct online classes without any difficulties. However, other teachers are concerned about the **downsides**[1] of the **proliferation**[2] of online teaching and learning.

First of all, conducting classes online is just untenable for teachers with young children at home. Take one of my fellow teachers, Mrs. Wang, for example. She was requested to stay home and teach her classes online due to the **pandemic**[3], and of course, her young kids and elderly parents were at home, too. Her online class sessions were often interrupted by her kids or other family members. She simply couldn't focus entirely on teaching and occasionally she even had a hard time hearing what her students were saying. That's why she thought conducting online classes at home was a **disaster**[4].

VOCABULARY

① downside (*n.*) 不利的一面
② proliferation (*n.*) 激增；多產
③ pandemic (*n.*)（疾病）大流行
④ disaster (*n.*) 災難

Another reason why some teachers don't like virtual classes is that when attending online sessions, students' attention spans are **noticeably**[5] shorter. According to research, the attention **span**[6] of students who spend a long time in front of a screen may be as short as ten minutes. I myself also notice that when taking online classes at home, the majority of students simply can't concentrate fully on the lecture. They may be easily distracted by small things on their desk, or even their **siblings**[7] and **parents**[8]. Therefore, I still think that traditional classroom learning is more beneficial for both teachers and students.

當然，有一些教師為他們能夠毫無困難地進行線上課程而感到相當自豪。然而，另有其他教師擔心著日益增加的線上課程其實有其缺點。

首先，對於家裡有小孩的教師而言，在線上上課是不可行的。我認識的一位教師，王老師，就是個例子。由於疫情的緣故，她被要求留在家裡並在線上上課。當然，她年幼的孩子和年邁雙親也都在家。她的線上課程經常被她的孩子或其他家人打斷，她根本無法完全專注於教學，甚至有時很難聽到學生們在說些什麼。這就是為何她認為在家進行線上課程是一場災難的原因。

有些教師不喜歡虛擬課堂的第二個原因是，在參加線上課程時，學生們的注意力明顯不足。根據研究，如果在電腦前待的時間過長，學生的注意力持續時間可能會短到只有十分鐘。我自己也注意到，在家上線上課程時，大多數學生根本無法專心聽課。他們可能很容易被書桌上的小東西，甚至受到他們的兄弟姐妹和父母的影響而分心。因此，我仍然認為傳統的課室學習對教師和學生都更有利。

VOCABULARY

⑤ noticeably (*adv.*) 顯著地
⑥ span (*n.*) 一段時間
⑦ sibling (*n.*) 手足
⑧ parents (*n.*) 父母

● **The reason [something] is that** … 〔某事〕的原因是……

⓵ The reason she started to learn Japanese is that she's seeking employment opportunities in Japan.
她開始學習日語的原因是她要在日本找工作。

Grammar

在正式的英文寫作中，提及 The reason ... is/was ... 之後須接 that。比方說：

⓵ The major reason the project failed was that we lacked sufficient funding.
那專案失敗的主要原因是我們缺乏足夠的資金。

但是，在口語中說 The reason ... is/was because ... 也是有人講且可以接受的。比方說：

⓵ The reason no one likes him is because he's so fake.
之所以沒人喜歡他，是因為他太假了。

注意，台灣英語學習者常說的 "the reason is because ..." 這樣的句子應避免。可改為 "this is because ..." 或 "the reason is that ..." 才道地。

Useful Tips

進行線上課程時，因距離與設備的隔閡，教師分配給每位學生的關注力的確不比在實體課室內的多。要解決此問題，教師應設計有吸引力的活動，或透過互動遊戲等讓學生有參與感。譬如使用 Kahoot! 做複習測驗，或請學生在 Padlet 上留言等，都是可以讓學生動起來不錯的方式。

我是學生
For
Students

線上教學的優點
Advantages of Online Learning

若是有在準備托福或雅思等英檢考試的學生，便能瞭解關於線上課程與實體課程的口語論述題屢見不鮮，下列句子及所運用的句型皆相當值得參考。

☐ I prefer online classes because I can view the **necessary**[1] **materials**[2] and assignments **digitally**[3] instead of carrying around **a bunch of**[4] books and papers.

我比較喜歡線上課程，因為所需要的講義和作業我可以看電子檔就好，而不用將一堆課本和書面資料揹來揹去。

☐ As a **reserved**[5] person, I enjoy taking online courses because I get nervous when I have to speak in front of a large group of people.

我是一個內向的人，我很喜歡上網課，因為這樣就不會像要在一大群人面前說話一般緊張了。

☐ Students do not have to travel to attend classes that **take place**[6] online.

學生參與線上課程無須在路上奔波。

☐ Online courses give me greater freedom to organize my **schedule**[7] and learn at my own **pace**[8].

線上課程讓我可以更自由地安排時程並按照自己的步調學習。

☐ If I have a question or issue during class, I can send a **private**[9] **instant**[10] message to the teacher.

如果我在線上課堂有疑慮或想提問，我可以傳即時私訊給老師。

TRACK **69**

☐ As an international student in Japan, I use Zoom to log in to the school system and have meetings with my Taiwanese classmates. **Distance**[11] is no longer a **barrier**[12].

我是在日本的國際學生，我都透過 Zoom 登入學校系統跟台灣同學見面。距離不再是障礙了。

Sentence Pattern

As a/an [someone], I [do something]. 身為……，我……

例 As a business major specializing in marketing, I plan to work at a marketing firm.

我在商學院主修行銷，我打算在行銷公司工作。

Useful Tips

線上課程的優缺點因每個人個性不同而異。以「線上課程缺乏面對面互動」這一點為例，對外向的學生而言可能是缺點，但對內向不喜互動的學生來說，反而是免去人際接觸的優點。因此在討論個人喜好時，就順著自己的論點說出合理的解釋即可。

VOCABULARY

① necessary (*adj.*) 必要的
② material (*n.*) 材料；資料
③ digitally (*adv.*) 以數位方式
④ a bunch of 一堆
⑤ reserved (*adj.*) 內向的；矜持的
⑥ take place 發生

⑦ schedule (*n.*) 日程表；進度表
⑧ pace (*n.*) 步調；速度
⑨ private (*adj.*) 私下的
⑩ instant (*adj.*) 立即的
⑪ distance (*n.*) 距離
⑫ barrier (*n.*) 障礙物；阻礙

線上教學的缺點
Disadvantages of Online Learning

筆者曾聽過不少學生分享,他們在線上課程上經歷過較大的「悲劇」通常是技術問題。例如麥克風故障、功能按鍵不熟悉,或因帳號密碼問題而無法登入線上教室等。然而,諸如此類的問題是在課程開始之前提早準備或測試便可預防的,因此不管是實體或線上課室,同學們都應預先做好「功課」喔!

☐ **From time to time**[1], I got disconnected and kicked out of online classes.

線上課程時不時會斷線,然後我就會被踢出虛擬教室。

☐ Well, an online class is not **suitable**[2] for all courses. I mean ... I just don't know the point of conducting a chemistry experiment online.

雲端教室並不適合所有課程。我是說……我真不知道化學實驗課在線上要如何進行。

☐ Taking classes online means fewer chances to talk informally with classmates. I still prefer to **interact**[3] with people **in person**[4].

上網課意味著與同學間聊的機會變少。我還是比較喜歡跟人面對面互動。

☐ Online learning means more screen time, and after looking at my laptop all day, my eyes are really dry.

線上學習就是要一直盯著螢幕看,整天看著筆電,我的眼睛真的很乾。

☐ For me, the number one disadvantage of taking classes online is dealing with **technical**[5] problems, like audio or connection issues.

對我來說,上線上課程的第一大缺點就是要處理技術問題,例如音源或連線問題。

⊡ TRACK **70**

☐ When I'm just sitting there in my cozy little room, I sometimes just lack the **self-discipline**[6] to stay engaged in online lessons and discussions.

坐在我那舒適的小窩裡，我有時會缺乏自律力，提不起勁參與線上課程和討論。

Sentence Pattern

● **Taking online courses means [something].**
上線上課程意味著〔某事〕。

　ⓔ Taking online courses means fewer face-to-face interactions with teachers and classmates.
上線上課程意味著和老師、同學的面對面互動會減少。

Useful Tips

雖說網路或技術問題仍存在，但也並非全無解決方案。舉例來說，學生因故無法參與線上課程，仍可使用其他工具（如 Snagit 等）將課程錄下以便稍後觀看。在現今科技發達的時代，加之線上課程也已成為不可逆的常態，若遇到類似缺點或問題，與其抱怨還不如盡力解決。

VOCABULARY

① from time to time 有時；偶爾
② suitable (*adj.*) 適合的
③ interact (*v.*) 互動
④ in person 親自；本人
⑤ technical (*adj.*) 技術上的
⑥ self-discipline (*n.*) 自律

討論線上教學的優缺點——學生視角

A: Hey, Matt. Did you hear that the Writing 101 course will be conducted online next semester?

B: Yeah. I think that it's a **terrific**[1] idea. I can attend class without even stepping out of my room!

A: Okay, it's certainly convenient. But sometimes I just can't concentrate on the lectures because of all the **distractions**[2] at home.

B: Really? Like what?

A: Well, like yesterday when I was taking an online class, my mom suddenly came into my room and asked me if I wanted some snacks.

B: Okay. That can be distracting.

A: And that's not all. I'm not sure if the Wi-Fi in my house is not stable or what, but I get disconnected all the time.

B: Hmm .... A bad connection can be a problem. Well, I guess you'd better find a quiet place with stable Wi-Fi to help your online learning go a little more **smoothly**[3].

A: You're right. And besides, these are **minor**[4] issues. For the most part, I **kind of**[5] enjoy all the benefits of virtual classes.

B: Yeah. Nothing is perfect, but I myself prefer **digital**[6] learning.

○VOCABULARY

① terrific (*adj.*) 極好的
② distraction (*n.*) 令人分心的事
③ smoothly (*adv.*) 流暢地；順利地

④ minor (*adj.*) 較少的；次要的
⑤ kind of（用於表示不確定）有點
⑥ digital (*adj.*) 數位的

A：嘿，麥特。聽說下學期的基礎寫作課程會在線上進行耶？

B：對啊。我覺得那樣很棒。我甚至不用走出房間就可以上課了！

A：是呀，當然是很方便。但有時我就是無法全神貫注聽課，因為家裡有很多事會讓我分心。

B：是喔？像是什麼？

A：嗯，就像昨天我在上網課的時候，我媽媽突然跑進我房間問我要不要吃點心。

B：的確。這可真會讓人分心沒錯。

A：還不只這樣呢。我不確定是我家的網路不穩定還是怎的，但就是很容易會斷線。

A：嗯……網路不穩確實是個問題。我想你最好找一個安靜且有穩定網路的地方，才能讓你的線上學習順暢一點。

B：妳說得沒錯。不過這些都是小問題。在大多數情況下，我還滿喜歡網課的好處啦。

A：對啊。沒有什麼東西是完美的，但我自己也偏好數位學習呢。

⊙ TRACK **72**

A: Hello, Joanne. This is Daniel. I'm calling to talk to you about the group presentation in our online class tomorrow morning.

B: Sure, Daniel. We've got our presentation files ready, so don't worry.

A: Well, I mean ... I'm not too familiar with those little icons in the Webex virtual classroom. Actually, I don't even know how to share my screen.

B: Oh, okay. It's actually pretty easy. On the main screen, you will see an icon with the word "SHARE" on it.

A: And what happens when I click on it?

B: You can choose to either share your whole screen or only a certain window.

A: Right. That doesn't sound too bad. I'd better log in to the online classroom a few minutes early and do some testing **in advance**[1].

B: Yeah, that's a good idea. Don't worry. After you **get used to**[2] one of these online learning platforms, you'll find that it's easy to start using others.

A: Well, I guess you're right. Online classes are part of the new normal, so there's really no other choice.

B: Exactly. Okay, so see you online tomorrow.

○ **VOCABULARY**
① in advance 預先
② get used to 習慣於～

A：哈囉，瓊安。我是丹尼爾。我打電話來是想和妳討論我們明天早上網課的分組簡報。

B：好啊，丹尼爾。我們已經把簡報檔案都準備好了，別擔心。

A：嗯，我是說……我對 Webex 虛擬教室中的那些小圖標不是很熟悉耶。其實，我甚至不知道要怎麼分享螢幕。

B：噢，OK。其實滿簡單的。在主螢幕上，你會看到一個上頭寫著「共用」字樣的小圖標。

A：點了之後會怎麼樣？

B：你可以選擇共享整個螢幕或只分享某個視窗。

A：好。聽起來不會很難。我看我最好提早幾分鐘登入教室先做些測試。

B：對啊，那樣不錯。別擔心啦，等你習慣使用一種線上學習平台後，你會發現其他的平台也很容易上手。

A：嗯，我想妳是對的。遠距學習已經是「後疫情新常態」的一部分，別無選擇了。

B：沒錯。那好，我們就明天在線上見囉。

線上教學的優點

Advantages of Online Learning

對於大專院校的學生，不論是畢業門檻、出國留學資格評鑑，亦或是職場面試審核，免不了有機會參與各式英檢考試，其中主要的托福 TOEFL／雅思 IELTS／多益 TOEIC 等檢定也多將寫作列為評分項目之一，而「傳統學習 vs 線上學習」這類可反映真實生活經驗的問題通常也是必考。

Example

As a **college**[1] student, I truly enjoy taking online courses.

First of all, online class sessions provide students with great **convenience**[2] and **flexibility**[3]. Instead of traveling back and forth between home and school, I can attend classes online and study at my convenience. For example, during typhoon season in Taiwan, universities may **cancel**[4] classes to **avoid**[5] putting commuting students at risk. At those times, I can continue to attend classes by logging into the school's online learning system or by watching recorded lectures at home. If we didn't have such convenient online courses available on the Internet, bad weather conditions would cause us to miss important class sessions more often.

In addition, various programs and courses offered by **top-notch**[6] universities around the world are available on the Internet. For example, I have always wanted to learn more about American history, but not much information is available in the library at my school. I searched for online courses, and was totally impressed by all the diverse American history classes offered by **first-rate**[7] universities in the U.S. By contrast, if I just took a normal course here in Taiwan, I would not be able to get such a comprehensive view of American history.

Online classes are more convenient, flexible, and **diverse**[8] than in-person classes. For these reasons, they are sure to be an important part of the education system for the foreseeable future.

身為大學生，我真的滿喜歡參加線上課程的。

首先，線上課程提供了極大的便利和彈性。學生不用在家裡和學校之間來回奔波，也可以方便地在線上上課和學習。比方說，在台灣的颱風季節，學校有可能會取消課程，以避免讓學生身處危險當中。這種時候，我便能在家透過登入學校系統繼續上課或觀看課程錄影檔。如果沒有如此方便的網課機制，學生可能會受到惡劣天氣的影響而錯過更多重要的學習機會。

另外，網路上還有世界一流大學所提供的各種研習。例如，我一直想多瞭解美國歷史，但我學校的圖書館中提供的資訊並不是很多。之後我搜尋了網課資料，我對美國一流大學所提供的各種美國歷史課程感到驚訝不已。相比之下，若我只是在台灣選一般的歷史課，我可能就無法學習到美國歷史的全面知識。

線上學習比起實體課程更加方便，有彈性也更多元。基於上述理由，線上課程在未來教育上可說是重要的必然趨勢。

Sentence Pattern

● **Instead of [doing something], S. + V.** 與其……，不如……

　例 Instead of staying home all day, you can go shopping with your friends.
　與其整天待在家中，你不如跟朋友出門逛街。

Grammar

Instead 與 instead of 兩者意思與用法皆不同，但許多人仍會混淆。

1. instead 一字為副詞，指「作為替代」、「取而代之」，可置於句首或句尾。
　例 Patrick did not concentrate on his homework assignments. Instead, he was distracted by his little brothers.
　派翠克沒專心地作功課，反而受到弟弟的影響而分心。
　例 I planned to go shopping, but I ended up staying home instead.
　我原本打算要去逛街，但後來還是待在家沒出去。

2. instead of 是介系詞片語，表「而非……」之意，後接名詞。
　例 He ordered a salad instead of a hamburger.
　他點了份沙拉，而沒點漢堡。
　例 Whenever I visit a new city, I always go sightseeing instead of staying in the hotel room.
　每當我造訪新的城市，我都會出門走走看看，而非僅待在飯店房間內。

○**VOCABULARY**
① college (*n.*) 大學；學院
② convenience (*n.*) 便利性
③ flexibility (*n.*) 彈性
④ cancel (*v.*) 取消
⑤ avoid (*v.*) 避免
⑥ top-notch (*adj.*) 一流的；頂尖的
⑦ first-rate (*adj.*) 一流的；優秀的
⑧ diverse (*adj.*) 多樣化的

線上教學的缺點
Disadvantages of Online Learning

各類英檢考試要求各不相同，比方說，TOEFL 要求三十分鐘內寫至少 350 字，IELTS 四十分鐘內須寫 250 字，且因紙本考試或電腦考試、打字或手寫的速度不同而異。但重要的是學生應先將自己的立場論點想清楚，如此不論是何種考試皆可立即回應並順暢寫出論述。

Example

Even though attending classes online seems rather convenient, some college students still prefer to avoid online courses. Here I **delve into**[1] the two most commonly mentioned disadvantages of online classes.

First of all, taking online courses requires a **certain**[2] **degree**[3] of self-discipline, yet students might feel less **motivated**[4] when learning online at home. For example, one of my classmates, Stanley, attended some electives online last semester. He told me, however, that he simply felt he was not getting sufficient **guidance**[5] from the **lecturer**[6], and **eventually**[7] he lost the **motivation**[8] to actively participate. Indeed, some students still prefer to interact with their teachers and classmates face-to-face. Online classes make many students feel **isolated**[9].

The second disadvantage of online classes is that students encounter technical problems from time to time. My personal experience can be a **vivid**[10] example. I attended a writing class on Google Meet last semester, and the course was constantly **disrupted**[11] by different technical issues, including audio, video, and even connection problems. **As a result**[12], the professor was **extremely**[13] busy **troubleshooting**[14] computer **glitches**[15] instead of focusing on delivering lectures and **leading**[16] discussions. In traditional classroom learning, teachers and students could simply concentrate on teaching and learning activities without worrying about technical problems.

Online learning makes it difficult for students to stay motivated and for teachers to maintain close connections with students. These problems are often made **worse**[17] by **unreliable**[18] technology. For these reasons, many students will always prefer in-person classes to online learning.

儘管線上課程看來是頗為方便，但一些大學生仍盡量不選擇線上課程。在此，我深入探討了線上課程兩個最常被提及的缺點。

首先，參加線上課程需要一定程度的自律力，但學生在家上網學習時可能會較不積極。例如，我的一位同學史丹利，他上學期在線上參加了一些選修課。然而，他告訴我，他認為他並無法從講師那裡得到足夠的指導，最終他失去動力，也無法積極參與課程。的確，有些學生還是喜歡與老師、同學面對面互動，而線上課程讓很多學生感到孤立無助。

線上課程的第二個缺點是，學生三不五時就會遭遇到技術問題。我的個人經驗就是個活生生的例子。我上學期透過 Google Meet 參與了一門寫作課程，課程被各種技術問題給打斷，包括聲音、影像，甚至是網路連線問題等。因此，教授焦頭爛額地忙於尋找解決這些技術問題的方法，也沒空專注於講課和帶領討論。在傳統的課室學習環境中，教師和學生就能專注於教學活動，而不必擔心技術問題。

線上課程讓學生比較不易保持動力，教師也不易和學生保持緊密的互動。這些困難點若再遇到技術問題的話，可說是雪上加霜。基於以上理由，許多學生仍偏好面對面的實體課程。

- **Even though S. + V., S. + V.** 即使……，仍……

  ⑩ Even though she is a professor now, she still attends seminars to receive advanced training in teaching.
  即便她現在身為教授，她還是參與講座以接受進階的教學訓練。

  ⑩ Even though he was not feeling well, he still went to work and hosted a meeting.
  雖說他身體不適，他還是去上班而且還開了個會。

Grammar

台灣的英語學習者常不自覺將中文「雖然……，但是……」直接代入英文句型中，而寫出 "Even though ... however ..." 這樣的錯誤句子。在此，我們複習一下這兩個字詞的個別用法。

1. even though 是從屬連接詞，其後為從屬子句，後應接逗號及主要子句。

   ⑩ Even though studying abroad may be challenging, I still want to give it a try.
   即使出國留學會充滿挑戰，我還是要盡力一試。

   ⑩ Even though it's raining, the boys still want to play outside.
   就算下著雨，孩子們還是想出去外面玩。

其中 even though 之後的 "studying abroad may be challenging" 是從屬子句，逗號之後的 "I still want to give it a try." 是主要子句。

2. however 是副詞連接詞，通常連接前後涵義對立的句子。

   ⑩ The trip to Japan was costly; however, it was worth every penny.
   去日本玩一趟頗貴，然而，這每分錢都花得值得呀！

   ⑩ I studied hard for the exam; however, I still didn't do well on the math section.
   我很認真準備考試，但數學還是考不好。

Vocabulary

① delve into 深入研究
② certain (*adj.*) 特定的
③ degree (*n.*) 程度；學位
④ motivated (*adj.*) 激勵的；有積極性的
⑤ guidance (*n.*) 引導
⑥ lecturer (*n.*) 講演者；（大學的）講師
⑦ eventually (*adv.*) 最終
⑧ motivation (*n.*) 動機；動力
⑨ isolated (*adj.*) 孤立的
⑩ vivid (*adj.*) 歷歷在目的；鮮明的
⑪ disrupt (*v.*) 打斷；擾亂
⑫ as a result 結果；因此
⑬ extremely (*adv.*) 極度地
⑭ troubleshoot (*v.*) 除錯
⑮ glitch (*n.*)（設備、機器等的）小故障
⑯ lead (*v.*) 引導
⑰ worse (*adj.*) 更壞的；更惡化的
⑱ unreliable (*adj.*) 不可靠的

CEFR 各類英檢成績參考對應表

教育部根據全球通用的語言能力評量標準 CEFR（Common European Framework of Reference for Languages 歐洲語言共同參考架構），列出全民英檢 GEPT、多益 TOEIC、雅思 IELTS 及托福 TOEFL 的對照成績，讀者可依此表參考自己的英文成績大致屬於哪個等級，藉此評估自我實力並訂定未來目標。

CEFR 語言能力參考指標	全民英檢	多益	托福			雅思
			紙筆	電腦	網路	
A1 入門級	—	—	—	—	—	—
A2 基礎級	初級	350+	390+	90+	29+	3+
B1 進階級	中級	550+	457+	137+	47+	4+
B2 高階級	中高級	750+	527+	197+	71+	5.5+
C1 流利級	高級	880+	560+	220+	83+	6.5+
C2 精通級	優級	950+	630+	267+	109+	7.5+

Notes

Notes

國家圖書館出版品預行編目（CIP）資料

雙語課室英文句典＝EMI in Online Classrooms／薛詠文著.
-- 初版. -- 臺北市：波斯納出版有限公司, 2022.04
　　面；　公分
　ISBN 978-986-06892-9-7（平裝）

　1. CST：英語　2. CST：遠距學習　3. CST：會話

805.188　　　　　　　　　　　　　　　　111002492

雙語課室英文句典
EMI in Online Classrooms

作　　者／薛詠文
執行編輯／游玉旻

出　　版／波斯納出版有限公司
地　　址／100 台北市館前路 26 號 6 樓
電　　話／(02) 2314-2525
傳　　真／(02) 2312-3535
客服專線／(02) 2314-3535
客服信箱／btservice@betamedia.com.tw
郵撥帳號／19493777
帳戶名稱／波斯納出版有限公司

總 經 銷／時報文化出版企業股份有限公司
地　　址／桃園市龜山區萬壽路二段 351 號
電　　話／(02) 2306-6842

出版日期／2024 年 7 月初版三刷
定　　價／380 元
I S B N／978-986-06892-9-7

⑬ 貝塔網址：www.betamedia.com.tw

喚醒你的英文語感！

Get a Feel for English !